Mystic Fool

by Andy Hill

ISBN-13: 978-1481993814

ISBN-10: 148199381X

www.mysticfool.com

To Jenny Ann, for all the goodness.

Chapter 1

Ripped away from an epic, phantasmagoric dreamscape, I yawned and groaned during several otherworldly seconds of knowing not where I was. As my eyes followed the fan spinning slowly above, my consciousness filtered back to the island of Koh Tao in southern Thailand. Rising from bed and sidestepping a phalanx of empty Chang bottles, I emerged to the front porch of the bungalow filled with desire, turning my ears to the sound of the sea and the breeze singing through the trees.

It was my twenty eighth birthday, and would be the beginning of a confused romp through a carnival of meaning, an attempt to stagger down the path of the hero, to catch the big fish.

Returning inside to put my clothes on, I remembered that I had to go find my shoe.

Padlocking the door, I retraced my steps down the paths adjacent the beach, stooping here and there to scan the grass on either side. I attempted to recreate the bizarre occurrence as best as I could remember it.

The night before, having just left a bar to go home and pass out, there were some women standing around outside. As I staggered past, one of them said "you wanna go have some fun, boss?" Paused in the orange glow of the lamp, I caught a closer look at her face, shellacked with makeup, and musingly asked "are you a boy or a lady?" At that her eyes grew wild, she shrieked and growled, grabbed my crotch, and lunged forward to rip the flesh from my face. Perhaps it was just her sense of humor, but in my altered state, she had morphed into a demon.

I tore off down the path, absolutely shitting myself, assuming she and her friends would follow all the way to my bungalow to make of my flesh a mutilated offering to sea spirits. As I was running, one of my shoes flew off, but it was a pittance to pay for my orifices remaining untouched by the moon-sick claws of this he-she-wolf. I made it back unscathed, locked the door, closed the windows, and laid in bed with a $3 knife I'd never used nor knew how, blacking into an inebriated, terrorized, slumber.

Back in the safety of daylight, I found the shoe at the base of some palms swaying forgivingly above and strolled to the store to stock up on the day's necessities.

The 7-11 was icily air-conditioned, and though I might wince at the rapacious spreading of American logos to such far flung places as the islands of southern Thailand, as soon as I stepped into the arctic wonderland inside, all my disgust at the supposed evils of globalization were quickly pacified. I glided over to the drink case and took my time deciding what to get.

With a fifth of Sang Som rum I headed back to my place to begin the festivities.

As I approached I could see Sean was on his porch trying to fix his hammock. I called over to him.

"Hey buddy!"

"Hey man- what's the crack?"

I told him it was my birthday.

"Well happy birthday, man! I see you've got a little birthday breakfast of champions for yourself there," he said, glancing at the rum.

"Mind if I join you?"

"Be my guest!"

I went down to get two glasses with ice and a bottle of coke from the bar. Returning to the porch, I sat down and poured us a couple of drinks.

"You know what I'd really like for my birthday?"

"Handjob?"

"I'd like to see a UFO."

"Oh, Jesus."

"I've wanted to see a UFO my whole life. Just once. And maybe go up in the ship for a few hours, fly around."

"You really think there are aliens out there?"

"You think there *aren't?*"

"Well, it doesn't seem all that realistic, at this point. I think they already would have made their appearance."

"What doesn't seem very realistic to me is that we'd be the only intelligent species in the infinity of space."

"How come we aren't living side by side with them, then? How come they haven't taken us to see their planets yet?"

"Maybe we are. Maybe they have."

"Yeah, but there's no proof of that. It's still the realm of sci-fi, blurry Youtube videos, corny television."

"True. Maybe there hasn't been enough of a...global occurrence yet for enough people."

"Yeah, and I think that would've happened by now."

"Well, we can't know at this point, so why should we automatically tend towards the conclusion that they aren't there?"

"Because you can't assume something's there just because you want it to be."

"You can't just toss out the past sixty years or so of the importance of the idea, though. Where does that come from?"

"Comic book authors. Hollywood."

"I'm not saying they'd necessarily be little green men with bug eyes. They could be made of light, or arsenic, or plasma, or things we have no conception of. Or, they could be remarkably like us. Who knows?"

"No one. That's the point."

"Well if a million other people have seen something in the sky that didn't behave like any known aircraft, I'd like to think it wouldn't be too difficult to let me in on that."

We made a couple of new drinks and put our feet back up on the railing.

"You know, most of the world's religions have stories about a being, or beings that came from the sky, and live in the sky. For instance, in Hindu mythology, gods came from the sky in flaming ships.

Is it crazier to believe in aliens than some kind of god? I don't see how believing in the common conception of god is any more rational than beings from other planets with a few more years' head start on building vehicles."

"Sure. I can't say I believe in either of them."

"I mean, we've never been to another planet, besides a machine on Mars and supposedly the Moon."

He turned in his chair.

"You don't think we went to the moon?"

"I have my doubts."

"You are beyond the pale, Ian."

"Hey, look at the facts. That's all I'm saying."

"Such as?"

"First of all- why haven't we gone back?"

"Ok..."

"It's as if after the first transatlantic flight happened, the engineers and scientists who made that possible just folded their arms and said 'alright, took care of that one' and stopped there. That's not how things work."

"Alright, what else?"

"Well, most people think that 'going to space' and 'going to the moon' must be close to the same thing, right? They're not even within the same realm of possibility. The average altitude for space flight is a few hundred miles. The International Space Station orbits at about 250 miles. You know how far away the moon is? Around 230,000 miles away.

"Then there's the small issue of the Van Allen Radiation belt, which begins around 400 miles and extends about 40,000 miles from the surface of the Earth. There is no way a human could go through it. They'd fry like a cat in a microwave. That's why we've never gone beyond it. All the footage we've seen was created in a studio lot probably somewhere in Nevada. Supposedly, after NASA saw Stanley Kubrick's *2001: A Space Odyssey*, they were so impressed that they had him do it."

He scoffed.

"Alright, well, even assuming they could pull off telling a lie that hard to contain, why would they risk it?"

"That's the simplest part. When the Apollo missions supposedly landed a man on the moon, it was 1969, the apex of the Cold War. The U.S. and the Soviets were the lone superpowers, trying to prove to the world that their brand was the best. What better way for the U.S. to show that to the world, as well as stick up the biggest middle finger in history to the Russians? You win the Cold War. You win over the world. Your brand triumphs. People tend to get a hard on about that sort of thing."

He leaned forward to make another drink.

"Well I tend to get a hard on about that girl we met on the boat from Surat Thani, and as luck would have it I saw her on my run this morning. She told me about some party on the beach she and all her friends were going to."

"Sounds like a hoot. Wanna head off soon?"

"Yeah I just need to do a few things online. How about an hour?"

"That works for me."

The sun was beginning its languid descent into the sea so I scampered out to the water and eased in, lying on my back with my hands behind my head. I gently kicked my feet, floating on the surface.

My entire life had been filled with an insatiable lust for the otherworldly. It was never that the grass was greener on the other side of the fence, but an entirely different color altogether. I never desired to remain where I came from, or to maintain the customs and worldviews I was brought up with. I had always longed to be in foreign places, among foreign people, doing foreign things. I wanted to go to the far ends of the Earth, into the bowels of the Earth, through the infinity of deep space. It might sound irrational, but it had always been the primary motive force in my life.

The idea of climbing a status ladder, gathering impressive toys, and planting my little flag in the dirt was what appeared foreign to me. From all my Bible reading as a youth, I resonated most with Christ's admonition against building my kingdom on Earth.

I saw myself as an archetypal Fool, roaming about, biding my time in this spectacle of time and space, amused and fascinated, lifted on sporadic arcs of insight. And on that special day, with Saturn coming back around, I knew I had to do something to initiate myself into this novel phase of my life.

With these considerations filling my mind, gently pushed back and forth on the surface of the water, I eventually swam back to the shore and returned to my room for an iceless cocktail and a shower.

After a little while I knocked on Sean's half-open door to find him hunched over his laptop. Closing it, he said "alright, mate. Ready-O."

We headed off to find the girl he wanted to prong. There was a party going on at a bar down the beach with a DJ spinning all the predictable music that you'd hear at every bar along the backpacker circuit that season. We found the girl and her friends from the boat, and I hung out and had a few drinks. I was, however, in no place to consider a pronging of my own for the evening. I had work to do. This had to be a day of initiation, of self-pronging.

After reaching my Black Eyed Peas limit, I found Sean and told him I was going back to pass out and that I'd see him in the morning.

"Are you serious? It's like eight!"

"I'm hammered, man. I've gotta go back and just pass out."

"Alrighty then! That's a hell of a birthday celebration! Don't hurt yourself getting into bed!"

I laughed, said goodbye, and traipsed back up to the path leading home.

Chapter 2

Back at my bungalow, I paced and thought about how to do something to ritualize my awareness of this cosmic, astrological shift. I went over what I knew about it.

The 'Saturn return' period is when Saturn comes back to the same place relative to the Earth that it was when you are born, roughly the ages 28-30. As I understood, it's a time of change, from one part of life to the next, whether we choose to be aware of it or not. Ideally, the old is swept away to make room for what is coming in the next stage. During our Saturn return we have a particularly clear vantage from which to take an inventory of our lives up until that point, of all the things we have and haven't done, to see our own trajectory.

I had been thinking a lot about alchemy, and the axiom *solve et coagula*. Dissolve and coagulate. Take it apart and put it back together. Analysis and synthesis. This was the general process that the alchemists would apply to base metals in order to transmute them into gold.

Everything in the universe is either in a state of dissolving or coagulating. Things come together and things fall apart. Cells, bodies, relationships, belief systems, cultures, empires, galaxies; all are undergoing vicissitudes imposed by these two states.

I was thinking of the alchemist's base metals psychologically, as the shadow, that repository of all shame, guilt, fear or things that just didn't fit into my nice idea of myself. Suppressed and alienated though it was, I knew it was a living part of me, and if I could confront and embrace it, I could free up an incredible amount of power. By doing so, a rift might be crossed, and an experience of oneness would occur as I accepted my own dark side.

I willed to dissolve this leaden burden and coagulate it back into myself, to incorporate it into my being. I understood that I had to cease being afraid of it, hiding from it, and projecting it out and finding it only in others. I didn't know what I was doing but I was led by a murky, intuitive sense. I wanted to reach down into the base of my being and somehow extract the gold from that within me I had been so afraid to embrace.

Saturn, lead, shadow, dissolve, coagulate. I said these words to myself over and over.

I wanted to own my shadow. I wanted to accept it like a prodigal son. I wanted to cook it and eat it.

Maybe it was all horseshit and wishful thinking, but I had an overwhelming feeling that it was important, so I went with that. It was like having to take a gigantic dump and knowing I couldn't hold it in any longer, because there might not be another toilet for a long time. I knew this would take weeks, months, maybe years, but I felt I owed it myself to initiate it then.

I sat down cross-legged on the floor and tried to breathe long, complete breaths. I slowly worked myself into a state like daydreaming, and visualized images of scabbed over, atrophied aspects of me, things I was ashamed of, scared of, falling away from my body. Also, the image of an old, repulsive hag covered in filth transforming into a beautiful young woman recurred in my mind's eye.

I imagined my arms extending and wrapping around my entire self, and pulling all that I was ashamed of close, to claim it, to embrace it, to become one with it.

This is it, baby, I said to what I imagined as the source of consciousness coiled within me. *Let's pump up the volume. I will go where you lead me, I will learn what I need to learn, I will change what I need to change, I will do what I must, but I'm ready to ride on the big waves now. No more running, no more allowing myself to be controlled by that which scares me, binds me, shames me, and weighs me down. Let's do this. Shoot me out of the cannon. Give it to me...*

I sat like that, slowly rocking back and forth, enflamed, until my legs were totally asleep and my back muscles were burning. I slowly rose, lit a cigarette, and sat in the middle of the bed, resting my eyes on the reflection of the moon across the surface of the sea. It was remarkably peaceful.

After several minutes, something caught my gaze outside the door. I leaned forward and saw the form of a large, black dog.

It slowly walked into the room and stopped. It stood there looking at me for several minutes. Something changed in the room. I couldn't feel if it was good or bad.

Slowly it climbed up into the bed, and I moved aside as it lied down beside me, facing the ocean as well. We sat there like that for what seemed like hours, in a strange, liminal state, suspended in the charged particles of the room. Eventually I laid down and passed out, the dog's head resting on my leg.

Chapter 3

I never imagined a place like Koh Phi Phi would be a popular Christmas destination, but it was throbbing with people. I arrived in the mid-morning on the 24th and checked into a large dormitory that looked like a homeless shelter. Dipping into the smaller side paths to avoid the herds, I cast about for a place to get some fresh juice for my parched, hungover aura.

I wanted to go on a boat trip to check out some of the surrounding islands. Dodging food stalls, kids playing football, dogs, and merchants selling all manner of trinkets, I went to hunt down a ticket. There were a million people selling boat trips of all kinds, and while I wasn't excited to go on a trip with twenty other people, I was by myself and it would be much cheaper to just get one of those group deals. I found one which was leaving momentarily and filed on with everyone else.

The coast of southern Thailand on the west side is in the Andaman Sea, and contains all these jagged rock formations that rise out of the surface of the water like the spires of a cathedral. It's one of the most unique and recognizable landscapes on the planet.

We made a stop to snorkel, and as I got back in I fished a warm Leo from my bag as a woman came walking up to me.

"Are you by yourself on this?"

"Yeah."

"So good to find someone on their own! Everyone is a couple, everywhere you go."

"I was thinking the same thing earlier. I've been by myself for two weeks now. Let's party. I could use some company."

"That's terrific, me too." She extended her hand. "Elise."

"Ian."

"Where are you from?"

"The States. Where are you from?"

"Brazil."

"You want a beer?"

"Ahhh- yes, a sip- I am still recovering from last night."

"Well, this is how you recover."

She smiled and took a drink.

I could already tell that she was high maintenance, the kind of woman who sends dishes back to the kitchen and puts her seat back in an airplane as soon as she sits down. But, she also looked like fun, if only for a day or so. I loathed traveling with people most times because I was so adamant about doing exactly what I wanted, when I wanted. But, she couldn't be all that bad, and it had been quite a long time since I'd sat and had a meal, or even a beer, with anybody.

We got to Maya Bay and it really was astoundingly beautiful, the pristine blue-green water enclosed by towering limestone. We decided to strap on some snorkels and check out the coral. After several minutes of circling around in the water, Elise came swimming up to me, very excited behind her mask, showing me some money under the water. We surfaced.

"Look at this!" She was brandishing a dripping 1,000 baht note.

"Did you just find that in your shorts or something? I love it when that happens."

"No I found it stuck under a rock! Can you believe it?"

"That's amazing! A Christmas present from the sea."

"Haha yes. How lucky!"

We treaded water for a few seconds and she asked me where I was staying.

"Oh, I'm staying at the dumpiest shithole on the island."

"Well, I have a guesthouse room, but it is too expensive, because they only had a room for two. You could stay there."

"That sounds fantastic. How much?"

"It is thirty. Too much for me. But if you want you can just pay ten."

"No, fifteen is cool."

"It is very clean, very nice, air conditioning, TV with the BBC and the CNN and a porch."

"I'll take it."

"Good!"

She swam a little closer to me and whispered in my ear, "and I have some of the LSD..."

"Wow...are you serious? That is a really, really nice Christmas surprise!" She was smiling devilishly.

"You like it?"

"I LOVE it. I want to marry it. I want to grow old with it."

She laughed and swam around.

"I think we should go back, some people are getting on the boat."

As she waded to the shore I stood there, facing the limestone walls that encircled the cove, the sun shining down as bright and blessed as ever, and thanked it that Christmas Eve, thanked it for all of its light, life, love, and liberty. And fun.

I scampered back to the boat and gave Elise a beer as the motor started and we headed back to Koh Phi Phi.

Chapter 4

"Oh Jesus, Ian...this place *is* a shithole."

I was putting the last of the things I'd kept in the locker at the hostel into my bag.

"I know. I feel dirty everywhere. Inside, outside..."

I gladly gave my key to the woman working the door on our way back down the stairs and into the sunlight. It was early dusk and the streets were less jammed than they had been during the day. We strolled along towards her place.

"We should stop and get some things for the room. Like alcohol."

"Yes. Like what? I don't want to drink beer all night."

"How about rum and coke?"

"Ok yes that sounds good."

I was able to sort out ice, cups, Sang Som, and bottles of coke, all on the way home.

Once we got back to the guesthouse she got in the shower and I made a drink while getting caught up on the BBC. It was a much nicer room than I was used to staying in, and I would have never in a million years stayed there had it not been for these delectable circumstances. But it wasn't *all that* expensive, just for a night or two.

She finally came out of the bathroom in a dress that looked like she was going to outer space, and asked me to make her a drink. I made us both one, taking mine into the shower.

I was so filthy I soiled the bathroom by showering in it. As I was toweling off I looked at all of Elise's bathroom stuff and it made me so glad I didn't have a girlfriend. What a pain in the ass, shlepping all that shit around everywhere! She had what looked like an entire 20 liter bag full of cosmetic supplies. It made me tired just looking at it. I put my jeans on, thankful for my freedom.

"Ahh that's better!" I took the towel out to the front porch to dry.

"Should we take the acids now?"

"Yeah let's do it."

She picked up a little plastic bag that was sitting on the lampstand and pulled out a small piece of pink cardstock, carefully tearing it in half. Looking at the two of them she said "you take the bigger one."

"That's nice of you."

"I don't need as much, believe me."

We held them up to one another like we were clinking glasses, in an impromptu blessing of the evening.

"To our evolution" I said.

"Yes, and Christmas."

"And Elise for supplying this sacrament."

"Ok...here we go..."

We sat in silence for a few minutes, really working them over, trying to get every last magical molecule out.

We had a couple more drinks and then she finally dragged me out to "the party." What she meant by that was another nondescript outdoor bar pumping horrible club music. She was very keen on dancing, and had been dancing around the room all night, but going out to one of those places sounded awful to me after eating acid. I wanted to hang out at the guesthouse and impress her with my intellect.

Eventually I relented and we locked the place up. She was dancing all over the street when we got out there, going right up to people and dancing with them. I was starting to feel pretty high myself, in a pretty reverential kind of way. I was blessing everything I walked by like a priest, while she was doing capoeira all over the place.

We floated into this place and she got someone to take a picture of us, but we couldn't stop laughing and made the guy stop for some reason. She immediately floated into the dance area and began bouncing around all over the place. I couldn't get in there though, I thought something was going to swallow me up, like it was the deep end of the pool, and I couldn't swim. The bar was like the side of the pool where I could safely rest and not worry about drowning in the lights.

She was trying to pull me in but I told her I seriously couldn't, and she eventually gave up. I had told her before we even left the guesthouse that dancing with me wasn't going to be possible. I told her I'd be right over there at the bar, and I'd be watching her. She smiled and moved her arms all over the place, the traces slowly fading in the air, and moved backwards into the froth of dancing people.

I walked to the bar, ordered a rum and coke, and planted myself. The glittering veil of matter around me made my eyes feel very rested. Soon I was picking out each individual and imagining their life stories. Every mannerism, every movement, every moment was like a data packet unfolding in my brain.

It seemed to be the perfect amount of compounds for the spectacle of the evening. I felt on top of it. I was aware of my own neurochemical processing as well as everything in my field of vision with perfect equanimity. An idea consumed me that this was the perfect, the absolutely gloriously perfect time to get a tattoo that I had wanted for a long time.

There was a parlour right on the path beside the bar that I had seen walking in. The idea was fixed in my mind.

I shuffled over to where Elise was dancing with another woman. I was kind of bouncing around, and shouted that I was going to be at the tattoo shop, pointing to it. She kept begging me to dance, talking about how amazing it was and spinning around with the other girl.

"I'll be over there, you can see it. Don't run off!"

"Of course not! I will come and see you in a little while!"

I walked over to the tattoo shop and spoke with the guy. We got it worked out and the price was good.

"That's perfect! Let's do it!"

I waited around for a little while until the chair opened up, then got situated.

The vibrations from the gun were actually kind of enjoyable, like a massage, an agreeable resonance throughout my entire body. After a little while Elise came over with a beer for me and bent down to see what it was.

"What does that say?"

"I love fun."

"Ian, you are sure you want to do this? How fucked up are you?"

"Yeah baby! I've been planning on this for a long time! I was just waiting for the right moment!"

She beamed and began dancing again, spilling beer on my foot and setting it down next to me.

"Do you need anything? Some food?"

"No, go on! I'll be over in a little bit. Almost finished."

She danced backwards towards the bar, back into the fold.

A while later he bandaged me up and I walked back over to the bar, where Elise was talking to a bunch of people. She was a real socialite.

"Ian, let me see! God you're covered in ink and blood!"

"Ahh it's just a little. I shouldn't have drank so much beforehand. But oh well! It'll be fine! What do you want to do?" She had a drink in her hand.

"Let's have some shots!"

We hung out at the bar for a few minutes with all these people she seemed to know already.

"I'm gonna dance for one more song!"

"Ok, take your time. I'm just fine hanging out right here."

"Dance with me!"

"No way! I never dance in front of anyone!"

She went off and I had another few cocktails, studying and enjoying absolutely everything with remarkable acuity.

Eventually she came over to where I was standing.

"Let's go find something else. You wanna go? I'm done here."

"I'm so over this place. Let me pay up. You want a shot?"

"Of course."

I downed my cocktail and grabbed us two shots of whiskey which we clinked and sent down the hatch.

We traipsed back out onto a path that led around the island. The events that followed are more like a bizarre chiaroscuro than any kind of narrative. At one point we were at a small, barely lit gathering of tables and chairs in the sand under some trees maybe twenty meters from the sea. There was a pool table that looked like someone had dropped a bomb on it, and an old Thai guy with dreadlocks dressed up as Jack Sparrow was sitting cross legged in the middle of it. He was telling us stories of his adventures on the sea and howling, and I easily convinced myself that they were absolutely true. After I complained that we had no rum with us he gave us a bottle he'd had in his house. It looked like it was a hundred years old.

Next I remember doing some kind of bizarre tai chi on the beach while Elise sat on the sand several meters down, talking to herself.

I also recall walking past a mosque and prostrating myself on the ground in front, with sacrosanct reverence, trying to initiate some kind of intra-dimensional communication, while Elise stumbled around begging to go home.

Then we were walking home and she was holding on to my arm for dear life the whole time. It was purely providential that we ever found our place. Out of nowhere she said "there" and it appeared, barely visible amidst the foliage.

I got the door open and the light on, and she passed out straight into bed.

I turned out the light and laid down to watch the movie playing behind my eyelids.

Chapter 5

When I woke I was filled with childish excitement at the light streaming in the window. I got up and took a leak, then gently pulled the bandages off the tattoo and took a shower. I was filthy and covered with sand from the night before.

When I got back inside Elise was stirring, moaning, and holding her head, her hair everywhere.

"Oh my god...it's like...it's like someone punching my head..."

I sat on the edge of the bed.

"Can I get you anything?"

Her face was half covered by her hand. "One of those coconuts. A cold one. Two of them."

"Alright, you got it."

She rolled over and I put a shirt on and tiptoed out the door.

I had a blissful, strange feeling, walking down the dusty footpaths. The psychedelic and straight worlds were blending back together again, and traces of the LSD caught my mind up in tiny eddies of curiosity.

I started to think about Christmas, and what it meant to me. It was obviously not the same holiday I knew as a child. I didn't believe in Santa Claus, I wasn't dressing a tree, my family was on the other side of the planet, and I had plenty of doubts about the historicity of Jesus.

How was I to place it in my sensorium, my experience? I couldn't just purge it from my mind or abstain from it like a curmudgeon. It seemed the wiser thing to just update my software and accommodate it in my own way.

The births of many near-eastern gods, such as Attis, Dionysus, Osiris, and Mithras, were celebrated on the winter solstice. They were worshipped primarily as solar deities, representing the power of the sun. During the six months following the spring equinox, the days got shorter until the winter solstice. At that point, the days began to get longer, and the return of the sun began, literally.

This is naturally a crucial day to agricultural peoples, whose entire lives were dependent upon this schedule for knowing when to plant and when to harvest their crops. It was celebrated symbolically as the birth of these solar deities, Jesus being one in a procession of them, who brought life to the Earth and its inhabitants.

At a deeper level, the symbolism of birth, death, and re-birth strikes even deeper to the core of human experience. When the ancients would see the sun rising in the morning, it was as if it were being born, and for all the common people knew then, that might have been the case.

At night, the sun would, in a similar sense, die. However, the most magical fact was that it was reborn the next, and every day. This formula of birth, death, and re-birth became an integral archetypal process to us, and in spite of our modern knowledge that the Earth actually revolves around the sun, causing it merely to look as if it 'rose' in the morning and 'set' in the evening, we still tend to be quite relieved when it does rise again in the morning.

This was the natural process that provided the fundamental mythos for Roman, Greek, Persian, and many other ancient cultures, and is still with us today. Birth and death remain the two events in human life at which we marvel at the mystery the most. They fill us with the most important inspirations that we experience.

This seemed to plant life in the barren field of my years of frustration at the skewed and confused celebration of this holiday. I was done being bitter and cynical at the traditions of others. It didn't do anyone any good. As Aleister Crowley said, "thou shalt not blaspheme the name that another knoweth God by."

So, while I was waiting for the guy to hack the tops off the coconuts, I decided that this would be the mythos and mystery that I enveloped myself in that Christmas. I would worship with vigor the Light, Life, Love and Liberty that the sun gives us all, and smile at the symbols of everyone else. Without the rebirth of the sun, there was no fun. And I loved fun.

I brought the coconuts back to the room to find Elise stirring. I set them on the lampstand next to her.

"Thank you, Ian. Oh god..."

"Do you want to sleep for longer?"

"No, no. I don't want to waste the day," she said laboriously, in between sips.

"That's the attitude. What do you want to do?"

"Well, we can get something to eat, first. And then go to the beach?"

"Alright, sounds good. I'm starving."

"Me too. Give me a little while. I need to recover."

"Do you need me to leave?"

"No, no, no...I'm just going to be very...slow today..."

I lowered myself to sit on the lampstand.

"That's fine, we got all the time in the world. Merry Christmas."

"Yes, Merry Christmas," she said in a hoarse voice, smiling.

* * * * * * * * * *

Elise took quite a while to regain full humanity but she was charming company. We tried to recall the events of the previous night and talked about our lives and passions. I played gopher for lunch, bringing back sandwiches and beers like a medic.

I took occasional dips in the sea and explored while she dozed in the sand. As odd as it felt to be on a tropical island for Christmas, I couldn't think of anywhere I would have rather been.

The sun continued across the sky and soon it was dusk. We walked back to the room to get ready for the evening's festivities. At the beach someone had told us about a place on the other side of the island called Bohemia that had fire dancing and Elise said "OH we have to go! I love watching it!"

After trekking about for the better part of an hour trying to find it, we eventually saw poi sticks spinning in the distance. There were all these little huts to sit in while watching different people take turns throwing all manner of flaming objects around in the air. It was insane. I had never seen anything like it.

We got pretty hammered at Bohemia and decided to leave after a couple of hours, knowing it would take us twice as long as it should to find the guesthouse. I picked up some ice on the way and when we got back I made us some fresh drinks.

"Ahhhh...I am so tired" she moaned, lying in her bed.

"Yeah, I'm beat," I lied.

Several minutes went by and she said "can you give me a hand massage? For some reason they are so sore."

"Sure," I said. The dull pain on my shoulder where the new tattoo was reminding me how incredibly awesome fun was.

I made a new drink, came over and sat on the edge of her bed, and began kneading the muscles of her hand.

Of course I was thinking about having sex with her. She was beautiful. But, I have found that if you are thinking about it, you will act like you are thinking about it. And if you act like you are thinking about it, you come off like every other dude, and I never wanted to come off like every other dude.

As an older friend once told me "Ian, you're the wolf. Now, you want her to smell the *blood* of the wolf. Not the heat."

Making sure it didn't seem like I was rushing it, I got up and went around to the other side of the bed, starting in on the other hand. After spending enough time on that one, I got up to take a drink.

"You want a back massage?"

"You are too nice..."

I gave her a massage and afterwards she moved over and took my hand. I slipped underneath the sheet with her and we began kissing. She whispered "do you have a condom?"

"I think so. Might be expired though. It's been a while." She laughed and I got up and searched through my bag to find it.

I got back into bed and she got on top of me. *It really has been a while, Ian. Please don't blow your load in five minutes.*

Fortunately the rum allowed me enough time for both of us to get to the finish line, just barely. Just barely is plenty, though.

She didn't seem to want to cuddle or talk about our lives, which worked out just fine for me. I got out of her twin sized bed to make myself a drink, and by the time I turned around, she was snoring.

I sat on the porch, drinking and listening to Thin Lizzy until I was ready to pass out.

* * * * * * * * * *

The next morning I crept out and got a couple of coffees and some fruit. When I got back she was flipping through the news.

"Oh, thank you. That's nice."

"I hope you don't need cream."

"No, this is just fine."

"Have a mango."

She asked me when I was leaving the island.

"Today. Around noon. I have a boat to Krabi and then a night bus back to Bangkok."

"Then where?"

"Siem Reap. I can't stay in Thailand beyond the day after tomorrow."

"I want to go to Siem Reap. I have a friend who lives there."

"Yeah it looks pretty amazing."

I kind of hoped she didn't want to come with me. She was a lot of fun to run around with, but I didn't always travel well with other people. Especially when they had so much luggage. It annoys me beyond reason.

"Well, maybe I can contact you when I am there?"

"Sure, definitely."

We exchanged contact info and chatted while watching the news for another hour or so, and I packed my bag. Hugging before I left, I said "thanks for a fantastic Christmas, Elise."

"You too, Ian. Safe travels, and maybe we will see each other in Cambodia."

"For sure. Be well."

I gently opened the door and slipped out.

Chapter 6

Getting myself worked into a seat on the smoldering bus from the Thai border to Siem Reap, a guy across the aisle asked "hey man, are you from Kansas?"

I was wearing a Kansas University jersey. I wedged my bag onto my knees and cracked an Angkor I had bought off a cooler behind the driver's seat.

"Yeah. Are you?"

"Yeah. Wichita."

"Ohh. My family's from Wichita. God."

"I know. Jesus, that place…"

He held out his hand.

"Russell."

"Ian. Nice to meet you."

The bus lurched forward.

"What are you doing in Siem Reap?"

"Just checking it out. No plans beyond the temples, and the town. You?"

"Same, I guess. Maybe find some work. Tomorrow we're gonna check out this organization that makes water filters with concrete, gravel and sand. They distribute them to people in the provinces. My buddy found out about it."

He nodded towards a guy sitting two seats ahead, who nodded at me, and I nodded back.

"That sounds really cool."

That night I got a room in the same guesthouse as the guys I met on the bus, one of whom had lived in Siem Reap the year previous and knew everything about it I needed to know. We smoked a couple of joints in their room and then went out and got royally pissed.

The next morning I shuffled into an internet shop, emailed the foundation, and got a phone call an hour later. One of the founders gave me directions and said I could stop by anytime, preferably before noon.

I slurped down some noodle soup on the side of the road and grabbed one of the thousand and one motorbikes hanging around. We sped east through town to the Crocodile farm, made a right, and then another right at the Angkor brewery about a half kilometer down. After a skip down a wide, dirt road, a flesh colored gate approached on our left, with a sign of the organization. I paid the driver way too much for the trip, thinking it cheap, and went inside the gates.

There was an office and several people milling about. I approached one and introduced myself as the guy who'd emailed that morning. One of them said hello and motioned for me to take a look around the place. Past the front area was a large garden with experimental-looking irrigation pipes, then a smaller area with large piles of sand, gravel, and sifting apparatuses suspended above and gathered about.

Just beyond was the area where the concrete was mixed and the water filters were built, finished, and stored before being distributed to local villages. Two Khmer guys were washing gravel and mixing concrete, while an intern sifted sand. Several others were doing some work with the pipes in the garden. There were a few dozen completed filters along a wall, waiting to be loaded into a truck and taken to a village. I asked Ted about volunteering.

"You can come in the mornings. They usually work from about eight until noon, and we can use any help we get. The more hands we have on deck, the more filters we can build."

We stepped outside and he asked "Didn't you mention that you had been teaching English in your email?"

"Yeah."

"Well there's a small English school just up the road that always needs volunteers. I'm headed up there now to drop off some stuff and I could give you a ride and introduce you to the woman who runs it."

"Sure, that'd be great."

He got his motorbike turned around and we were off. Continuing down the road the foundation was on, we eventually turned off onto a small dirt path that wound past houses made mostly of scraps of wood and corrugated sheet metal. Angling around buffalos and families of chickens, we arrived at a small gate over which one could hear the sound of children laughing and playing. We got off the bike and walked in.

There was a playground set, a small house, and a row of three classrooms made of bamboo and thatch. Kids were playing and jumping around, paying us little attention while several adults helped a few children working on homework at some tables. We walked up to the house and Ted knocked and slowly pushed open the door. A Cambodian woman got up and greeted us. Ted introduced me and said I might be interested in teaching.

"That's great. We always need teachers. Will you be here long?"

"I'm not too sure, I just got here last night."

"Well, we have classes in the morning and the afternoon, at nine thirty and two thirty. They're two hours long. We have more need in the afternoon, as a couple who was with us last month just returned to Australia."

A little boy ran up to me and stuck his hand out for a high five.

I put my hand out. "Hey buddy."

He grinned, shrieked, slapped my hand, and ran off.

"When did you want to start?"

"I suppose I can start whenever."

"Ok well we don't have classes tomorrow or Sunday, so Monday?"

"Sounds good."

"Ok, two fifteen would be good."

"Great. Sounds like a plan."

I was then conscious that I was wearing a sleeveless jersey, cut off shorts, and my tattoos were all showing.

"Oh, I can wear a nicer shirt and pants."

"No, don't worry, it's fine. Don't wear anything nice because they'll be scared to play with you. What you have on is just fine."

"Ok, that works for me!"

She smiled and shook my hand, and I said I'd see her on Monday.

"You remember how to get back? I'll be here for a little bit and I don't know if you want to wait," Ted said.

"Yeah, no problem. Nice to meet you both! Take it easy."

I dodged a group of girls running by to one of the classrooms and stepped out of the gate back onto the path leading to town.

Chapter 7

I was excited to have some structure to my day and decided that it would be a fine idea to stay in Siem Reap until my visa ran out. After only a day, I already knew I really liked it there. It was quaint, like a small town, and I was surprised by how at home I already felt, having explored the French Quarter enough to get a feel for the vibe the night before. No doubt it was touristy, as Angkor Wat was fifteen minutes away, but it didn't seem overwhelmingly so.

Walking back to town I got some more soup at a street stall and thought about finding a place to live. The bar I had been at the night before seemed to be the best place to start looking. There were plenty of semi-permanent expats hanging around who would most likely know about rooms to rent.

That evening I went around to one of the bars I'd been the night before and perched at the bar, intent on finding something cheaper than my $8 a night room. I'd take anything with a toilet, a window, and a lock on the door. After a couple of Angkors a guy came in and sat next to the guy who was next to me. They were talking about different properties in town that they were looking at buying, and the legalities of it. I butted in and asked if they knew anything about how to find a place to rent for a month or two.

"Sure, mate. Uh...can you meet me tomorrow around two? I can take you around to a couple of places my girlfriend knows about."

"Yeah, perfect."

"Ok great, see you then. Oh, what's your name?"

"Ian."

"Will, mate." We shook hands and he went back to talking to the other guy.

I drank and shot the bull with the bartender for a little while before going out to explore.

Walking over to another bar, I saw Russell sitting out front and he waved me over. We went inside and sat down at a table, and he pulled out a bag of weed and began rolling a spliff.

"Really? Right here?"

"Yeah, that's the deal with this place. Everyone does it here. Not an issue at this bar, as far as I can tell."

"This is the kind of freedom that people back home just have no clue about. If we were in the States we'd have to show our IDs to get a beer! Can you imagine?"

As our brains expanded the conversation turned to matters less mundane.

"So I'm with this girl last night, and after we made it she starts laying these tarot cards out and saying she wants to 'do a spread with me.' So we sat on the bed and she did this kind of grounding thing where she began chanting these words, like 'om' and shit, holding both my hands with her eyes closed. It was pretty far out."

He re-lit the joint, took another hit, and passed it to me.

"So what happened?"

"She begins laying the cards on the bed and then sits and stares at them for several minutes, kind of studying them. Usually I'd just roll my eyes and politely pick up my things but I figured I'd just trip out on it. And, we were ripped."

I handed him the joint.

"Well did she have anything interesting to say?"

"Remember how I told you about how I left Koh Phangan with all my dive gear and was looking for where to go next, and how I didn't know whether I should go back to the States or settle out here and teach again?"

"Yeah."

He put out the joint and began breaking up more weed in the same motion.

"Well she told me to think of a question or a situation in my life I wanted to understand more, that I wasn't allowed to tell her. So, I was thinking about this situation with my ex in Koh Phangan, that a lot of my shit is tied up with right now. She said the way the cards were set up was supposed to tell a kind of past, present, future scenario."

He took a drink.

"And, it's not like she blew my mind or anything, but it threw some light on the situation down there. I mean, my ex wanted to stay there and open up a bar, but I didn't think I could because it was so fucking small and I'd already been there for a couple years and wanted to move on. Last night, whatever it was, just got me thinking differently about it all."

He shook his head and kept breaking up the weed, then stopped.

"Then she said I had a major decision to make in my life and said there was a card in a place that's supposed to spell the future of that situation. She said I needed to make sure I was doing the right thing and all this stuff. And all of that seemed pretty right on, you know? I mean it at least got me thinking differently about Koh Phangan."

"What was the card she was talking about?"

"Uhhh, lemme look." He flipped through a journal that was sitting on the table with one hand, his other hand holding the nearly-rolled spliff.

"The Hanged Man."

"Ok..."

"And I'm not saying I'm into all that stuff, tarot and horoscopes and fortunetelling and all that, but it was pretty interesting. I'd never had a chick do that kind of shit with me before. It was a trip. She was a freak."

He lit the spliff and passed it to me.

"What do you think about that stuff?"

"Well, I'm as averse as anyone to new age cheese, but I've studied the tarot pretty seriously before and I think it's a lot more interesting than some kind of fortunetelling device."

"Yeah?"

I took a drink of my beer.

"Well, it's like a wordless book, right? I mean, that's how I think of it. And we don't really know where it came from. I mean, we don't know where the scheme came from, the images or the order they're in. So, for some reason, there's this set of images that definitey aren't accidental, and seem to be conveying something about a process, like the scenes in a movie or something."

He nodded. We were both totally stoned.

"I think of them as archetypes. I also think that to understand the tarot, you don't go to someone and say 'here, set these cards out and tell me what's going to happen in my life,' because A, my cynicism moves me to think they'd just tell me what they think I want to hear. And B, and this is the real reason....you gonna pass that?"

He had been sitting there red-eyed, the joint just burning down in his hand.

"Oh shit man, here."

"Not to be a dick-"

"No, no, I can't stand that shit when other people do it."

"And B, the real reason is that I think the tarot has to be approached as almost a living thing, and can only be understood by really taking the time and meditating on the cards, because they open up things within us that allow us to understand our own reality with more...clarity, I guess. They're not there to like, tell us things, like a ticker tape, but they begin a dialogue within us, and between us and the world around us. They allow us, through a kind of inner unfolding that only comes with patience and reflection, to see the world and the things going on in our world as evolving like...like a narrative."

I realized I'd been standing on the joint.

"Woops" I said as I handed it back.

"I read someone say once that a person could learn all they needed to know about life just from the images and symbolism in the tarot, and it would suffice like if it were the only book you had on a desert island."

"Yeah, people say that about the Bible too."

"Very true. But, I think the symbolism on the cards speaks to a realm of our consciousness, call it the unconscious, which is beyond words, and beyond the logic we use in everyday life. If we allow it to transcend our normal consciousness and look at them as the mysteries they are, they can enter into a kind of dialogue with our unconscious, and things begin rising to the surface of our waking, normal life consciousness, and we begin to understand our lives in novel, hopefully more creative ways. Its not just straightforward information, like the words in a book, you know? Its like a living, intelligent system. I mean, it can be. Like anything, you gotta try it out. Use the scientific method. Poke it and see what happens."

"Huh." He pulled one last hit off the spliff and pushed it out in the ashtray.

"So what's up with the Hanged Man card? You want another beer?"

"Of course." We signaled to the bartender.

"Well, I don't trust my knowledge at this point, it's been a little while, but the Hanged Man is kind of like being strung up, or trapped in a situation, and also kind of like sacrifice. Almost like a person hanging on a cross. So, that could speak to a situation, in your case between two people, where maybe one is suspending their life, or putting it on hold, or sacrificing for the other."

"Maybe me staying in Koh Phangan."

"Well, maybe. But also-"

The lady brought our beers over and set them on the table.

"But also what I've always seen in that card is that the guy's upside down, and it's like...he's seeing everything from a different perspective than the other people standing around, and a perspective that's definitely new for him, you know?"

He nodded and sipped at his Angkor.

"So, it's an obstacle, for sure. But it doesn't have to be a bad one. To me it always meant misfortune coupled with a new perspective on things."

"Interesting."

We sat for a little while, enjoying the high. He spoke again.

"Well I've just been thinking about it a lot and some things are hitting me that I didn't really see before, when I was in Thailand dealing with all of her shit and my own frustrations. I think in some way that girl pulling out those cards last night just jolted me. I don't think it was the fact that they were Tarot cards or that she was really seeing into my situation or anything...I just woke up thinking about it differently."

"Well, that's always good."

"Yeah..."

We sat in silence for a few minutes, watching people walk by.

"You want to play some pool? The one in the back just opened up."

"Yeah, man, I'd be down for a game. It's been a while though. I'm pretty shitty."

"It's ok this isn't ESPN2."

We hung out for an hour or so more when he got a phone call.

"It's that girl, I'm gonna go meet up with her at her guesthouse. You could totally come if you want."

"Ahhh its cool, thanks though. I'm gonna head home soon anyways. I'll see you around later, maybe here tomorrow night."

"Yeah, I'll be here. See you then, man."

I went back to my room, had a few rum and cokes, and paced up and down the room, processing the events of the day.

After that conversation with Russell at the bar, I had the tarot on my mind.

When I began studying the tarot I realized that there was a kind of algorithm, a sequence of stages within it through which a character travels. That character is the card numbered zero, the Fool.

Through the cards of the major arcana, the trumps, of which there are twenty two, the Fool travels along a journey beset by various triumphs and tragedies. The trump cards represent these different phases of his adventure. In a sense, the Fool is a hero-in-the-making. By studying and meditating on the meaning of the trump cards, we become more aware of the different things that we might experience in life.

For instance, the Lovers card can represent when a person chooses something in their life, such as a lover, over the safety and confines of the home or parents. The Hermit card represents a time when we retreat from the world of external responsibility, and withdraw into our inner world, to reflect, away from the expectations of others. The Death card represents a time when something in our life dies, such as a relationship or a career, and we need to be able to see when it is indeed dead and must be mourned and released. Of course, when we have come to grips with the reality that something in our life has reached it's shelf life, it is then that we have cleared the space for something new to grow in it's place.

But the archetype of the Fool is one of the most fascinating things about the tarot. As the first (and the last) card, numbered 0, the Fool contains the entire deck wrapped up within itself.

The Fool represents the essential, and our innermost desire to move towards a sense of oneness, of infinite opportunity, and a working reconciliation with the world around us. This process is aided by the continuous searching, risking, failing and searching and pushing on again that is inherent in the path that the Fool treads. With his lilted gait and shoddy shoes, the Fool's seeming carelessness pushes him to frontiers beyond the pale of known things.

He has the audacity to wonder what is beyond the horizon, beyond the bounds of the consensus, orthodox worldviews that permeate his paradigm. His quest is to seek and understand his own true nature. It is there that he finds the connection between himself and the furthermost reaches of the universe. The cards represent all the opportunities in human experience to do this.

What I desired was the realization of my essential nature, and it was my primal fear that I should wake up one day and realize that I sacrificed the essential for the tangential.

I eventually passed out with the glow of the BBC illuminating the room.

Chapter 8

The next morning was delightful. I awoke early. The powers that be prohibit me from sleeping past seven on most mornings. I walked into town to see where I could get some breakfast.

There was a little French place where I had a croissant and a cup of black tea for a scruple. It was a very pleasant scene and reenergized my desire to stay in Siem Reap for longer than the handful of days I had originally planned.

After paying I walked around town, to my delight finding a general store of sorts, which had copies of the International Herald Tribune, stamps, stationary, books and liquor under one roof.

After some more wandering, I got to the bar and had a beer with Will and his girlfriend before she took us over to a house about ten minutes' walk from the middle of town. A family lived on the first floor but it didn't seem as if anyone else was on the second or third floors. They showed us up to a room on the third and I didn't have to deliberate internally for longer than five seconds in deciding to rent it. It had corner windows, a fan, a TV with cable, and a private bathroom. The family who owned the house seemed nice and unconcerned with my living there.

"How much?"

Will's girlfriend talked back and forth with the woman that had shown us the room and she said "sixty dollars."

"A month?"

"Yes."

"I'll take it."

We exchanged pleasantries, I gave them the cash, they gave me a key, wrote down the wattage displayed on the electrical box, and told me I would pay the bill at the end of the month. It was that simple.

Will and his girlfriend seemed very happy that it all went off as planned, and he asked if I wanted to go back to the bar with them.

"Thanks, but I think I'll go back and check out of my guesthouse and move my things over."

"Sounds like fun! Well, see you later, Ian, I'm sure at Warehouse later on. There's some kind of costume party tonight if you're interested. Should be a good time!"

"Ok sounds good, Will. Thanks again."

I thanked his girlfriend who was chattering away on her phone and we parted ways on the dusty dirt road under the piercing sun.

I repacked my bag at the guesthouse and was out. I got a kick out of the fact that the guy running the place stayed in his hammock while I paid him for the two nights I was there. He fished my change out of the fanny back between his legs, smiled, and went back to sleep. When I arrived at my new house the family acted as if I had always lived there, and just smiled and continued hanging their laundry up in front of the house.

I walked in and felt like doing something ceremonial but I just set my bag down and stood in front of the window, studying the view. It was nice. There was a large grassy area crisscrossed with walkways behind the building, and palm trees everywhere. I flopped down on the bed and turned on the BBC while I rolled a joint and enjoyed my new digs.

After a little while, I thought about how I needed to get my meditation practice back into regularity. It's strange that if I neglected it I would feel guilty about it, like a person who hasn't been to confession in a long time. Stranger is the fact that I had to either ignore or overcome the idea that there was the chance that I might be doing it only out of this petty sense of guilt. And, I had to make sure that the entire thing wasn't just a way to stroke my ego, make myself feel better, or score cosmic brownie points. How could the practice of simply sitting on my ass and quieting my mind evoke such insanity?

Brushing all of that aside and hoping it was nonsense, I switched off the TV and folded up several shirts, placing them in a stack on the floor. I fished my cell phone out of my bag and sat down on the little cushion of shirts, cross legged.

I set the alarm on my phone for ten minutes ahead, placed it beside me, straightened my back, and closed my eyes. I felt good for a little while, then started thinking about how long it had already been.

It has to have been at least three minutes, but it feels like ten. Probably means it's only been two.

I began to sweat. A bead of sweat was creeping down my forehead.

You're not supposed to wipe that off. The whole point of asana being the first of the eight limbs of Raja Yoga is so that you can learn to ignore the stimuli coming from the body, to learn not to be distracted by that little bead of sweat.

I wiped it off. My back and groin muscles were complaining, and my ankles were falling asleep.

It was common for me to sit down and begin a session, and then in the first minute or two, scroll through the rolodex of images, sacred sounds, motifs, to try and figure out just what I should focus on.

What am I supposed to even be thinking about? I've read how many books about this, and practiced it how many times, to what end?

It was getting really hot.

I should have put the fan on full blast before I sat down. Idiot. Is it ok to get up and turn it on? Does that constitute a break? I'll feel bad about it. I should just sweat it out, I know. But how can I begin to concentrate when I am being cooked alive in this room on the most breezeless day ever? I'll sweat it out. I have to be able to make this. It's only ten minutes, for Christ's sake.

About eleven seconds later I quickly got up and turned the fan on full blast, and angled it more accurately at where I was sitting. Since my legs were asleep, I almost fell in my scramble back to the seat, which I tried to assume as fast as possible, as if someone were watching.

Pathetic. You'd last less than a day in one of those temple stays. You'd make the shittiest monk. Aren't I supposed to be actually concentrating on something, anything? Ok. Red triangle. No, circle.

In my mind's eye, a faint circular blob grew huge, then tiny, then disappeared, then kept moving around, amorphous, barely visible against the blackness.

How can I keep doing something that won't happen in the first place? How long has it been? Maybe my cell phone ran out of battery, or I set the alarm to AM, accidentally? That would suck. But, I shouldn't check it.

I checked it. Two more minutes to go.

Shit. Woops! Am I really capable of doing this every day? How many hours fly by when I am just pacing around this place, talking to myself? And I can't just sit for ten minutes? I've got a long way to go. I can't wait to get a beer after this. And masturbate. When I'm finished I'll go out and get a beer, come back up and masturbate. That'll be great.

I blasted through the remaining, hellish minute, counting every second until the alarm went off, still wondering if it had run out of power.

Smooth sailing...we can do this...ok...woah...I'm feeling kind of trippy, kind of weird. That's good. I think a few seconds went by there when I didn't think about what I was doing. That's go-

The alarm went off and I instantly relaxed, my legs completely asleep, my lower back and groin screaming, my entire body covered in dripping sweat. I then went out, got a beer, opened it on the way back up the stairs, flopped onto the bed, and masturbated.

Chapter 9

I was very happy with how busy I was keeping myself. In the mornings I was working and trying to learn as much as I could about making the Biosand water filters. It was a remarkably simple and cheap process, given that the end product took ground water and produced up to forty liters an hour of pure water for years and years.

The responsibilities mostly included washing the gravel and sand that would be used to make the concrete as well as to put inside the filters. There was also mixing and pouring concrete, taking the molds off, and finishing them.

Around noon I would head back into town and grab some noodle soup or something equally cheap (my lunch budget was set at $1) and usually swing by the Angkor Famous, a comparatively less touristy cafe in an alley in the French Quarter. All of their drinks were $1 so I would usually have a couple, then swing back by the apartment, change into less destroyed clothes, and walk back out to the outskirts of town to the school.

Teaching there was a trip. The kids were so enthusiastic and happy to be there, and worked really hard. They were probably some of the best students in the world to teach. I never had to ask any of them to be quiet.

It was in Siem Reap that I first encountered real poverty. Walking daily through that village where people took showers in front of their houses with a bucket of river water, lacking access to electricity and many of them to basic sanitation, people didn't seem run down, like their soul was afflicted by their need. It took me aback and caused me to see things a little differently.

On one occasion, a few boys from class were walking with me down the path in the direction of town to their houses. When one of them got to his house, which was a box of scrap wood and plastic, he told me to wait and scampered inside. When he came out he had a cardboard New Year's decoration, which had to be one of the only things in the house, and gave it to me. In the end I couldn't accept as I felt bad taking it, but his family came out and chatted with me and gave me some mangoes in a little plastic bag. I was blown away by that.

Many of the students were orphans, and many were infected with HIV. Knowing these things while seeing their boundless buoyancy and optimism was overwhelming. I would hurry home through the town so I could sit on my bed with a drink and sob my face off for about an hour. It was disorienting, and it took a little while before I was able to understand simultaneously their tragic circumstances and their natural joy. I had to evolve some paradigms.

My daily schedule worked more or less like that for the month I was in Siem Reap, and my situation was helped out considerably by a nightly gig at a wine and tapas bar which handed me all the drinks I wanted from eight to midnight and a $10 bill in my pocket. This was more than enough to pay for my daily allowances, including room and board. I felt blessed.

I tried to live a pretty normal life there. I had friends I would see in the evenings at the same several bars, and projects going on during the day that I was excited about being involved in.

I also continued to drink like a fish. In spite of all the novel, memorable, and celebratory experiences I was having, I was still as sorrowful as ever at the injustices I saw everywhere in the world. I kept myself buzzed throughout the day because it was a kind of protection against that sorrow. It was like erecting a glass wall which stood between me and all of the things that made me sick about the past and current state of the planet.

I thought I was pretty invincible. I never had anything resembling a hangover because I never took a break long enough to. Withdrawal doesn't occur when it's always with you. This sense of invincibility was soon to be punctured, as was the lining of my stomach.

From a metaphysical perspective, you could say that my anahata chakra, which governs the personal will, ambition, and sense of self-control, had been neglected and abused for years. From a physical perspective, a peptic ulcer, the relatively mild symptoms of which I had held at bay for some time, had been neglected and abused for years.

I awoke one morning with an agonizing pain just below my solar plexus.

Any tiny movement exacerbated this, but I was forced to squirm as any position I happened to lay, sit, stand, or lean in was equally awful. Filled with nausea, I leaned over to get the water bottle that was beside my bed. After taking a liberal set of chugs from it, I laid back down, shaking and sweating, and felt it all coming right back up.

I ran to the bathroom and was able to make it to the door, my feet and hands holding me steadfast in the frame. Vomiting violently, an electrical shock of pain shot out from my stomach to my entire body, and a geyser of reddish, liquid puke spewed all over the sink, toilet, and floor. I almost collapsed and held the door frame, looking at all the blood and what looked like small pieces of purple colored tissue, evidently pieces of my stomach lining.

I vomited and heaved several more times, each one causing a shock throughout my body that would have made me collapse if I hadn't the door to hold onto. There was no way of directing it into the toilet, or anywhere. I could barely stand.

Finally, struggling to breathe, the worst of the nausea subsided enough for me to stagger, hunched over, and crumple back into bed.

I had heard people talk about ulcers, placing their hand on their stomach and saying they couldn't eat spicy foods or drink coffee, but this beast was a different species. I had no specific knowledge of what was going on inside of me at the time, but I was pretty sure that I was at the point where one traditionally goes to a hospital. This was no fever, flu, or food poisoning. It felt as if the villain from *Indiana Jones and the Temple of Doom* had reached into the area about an inch south of my sternum, and was clutching and twisting whatever was in there.

I was terribly thirsty. I drank some more water, instinctively drinking huge amounts. Several minutes later, I ran in and vomited again, equally bloody, with a metallic and decrepit smell and taste. I had never thrown up this spasmically or uncontrollably before. My adrenaline was shooting out of my ears and I was shaking intensely.

Back in bed, I sat on the edge, because to lay down even halfway seemed to stretch my stomach out too painfully. I had never been so acutely aware of pain. My consciousness was focused so directly and painstakingly on the tremors coming from my stomach that every second was its own eternity of agony, like a hot iron shoved carnally about in my upper torso.

My thirst mounted, and became of a different kind than I had ever known. I sensed it less in my mouth and throat than in my guts, and actually felt like I was drying up. Every time I tried to drink some water I would end up lurching back to the bathroom for another volcanic outburst of watery, bloody mucus. It was several hours before I realized that I could take no more than a small mouthful at a time, as the vomiting that would inevitably follow was too cripplingly painful to think of enduring.

And I knew that it was entirely my fault.

Out of respect for the transcendent intelligence that sustains the universe, I never thought or uttered the sentiment "if you make this go away I swear I will never, ever touch booze again," because we both knew it would probably be a lie.

The shivering, sweating, squirming, vomiting and groaning continued for three agonized days and nights. I was in far too much pain to sleep, and completely averse to the thought of even a morsel of the blandest food. All I could do was lay in bed and count the seconds between mouthfuls of water and the need to run to the bathroom. It was like my body was grinding absolutely everything out of itself, including pieces of itself, as the stomach lining would continue coming up occasionally.

By the end of the second day I was well enough to walk, hunchbacked and slobbering, down the stairs and across the street to get a bottle of water. By the fourth morning after I had woken with the sickness, I was well enough to get a plate of white rice from across the street and eat it slowly, carefully chewing each bite into a creamy paste before swallowing.

It was incredible to be able to drink as much water as I wanted. But, the pain of those four days and nights faded from my mind much quicker than wisdom would dictate. I plaintively assured myself that I should probably only drink beer from then on.

To a saner person, this bout with illness would have been more of a wake-up call. I stubbornly swept it under the rug. I figured that it wouldn't happen for a long time and by then I would have medicine and maybe professional advice. Or I would have some milk. That was the insane logic that I used to justify continuing to drain bottles of rotgut whiskey. I never thought that I would quit drinking. That was a prospect that simply didn't fit into my worldview, and the wetness of my brain provided for a remarkable amount of elasticity of what was and wasn't possible.

There was no one around that I'd known for more than a couple of weeks, but rum was an old friend, and I knew that living without it was something I'd never care to do. So, after I felt normal again, I went on with my daily routine, and assumed the universe would let me get what I wanted out of it before my stomach would completely disintegrate.

It was also appalling that with all of my focus since my birthday on things I needed to let go of in my life that had held me back, on dissolving the decayed barnacles prohibiting my evolution, I was able to keep that searchlight from playing across this issue. I was able, somehow, to be aware of everything else that might be holding me back, like conceptions of things I'd learned as a child, or antiquated social expectations. But, I was able to repress the immediacy of the fattest elephant in the room.

I was soon down to my last several days in Cambodia, and I needed to press on to Vietnam. I took a bus down to Phnom Penh to get my visa and was on a bus to Ho Chi Minh City the next night.

Chapter 10

I had the fortuitous timing to arrive in Vietnam during the culmination of the celebration of Tet, the Vietnamese new year. For Vietnamese, Tet probably has the importance of all the Western holidays rolled into one. Families spend time remembering their ancestors and offering to them incredible amounts of food, liquor, cigarettes, and whatever else Grandpa used to really enjoy. The items are placed on the family altars that are ubiquitous in Vietnam, and after a mystical period when their essence passes on to the ancestors in the spirit realm, they can then consume them.

This timing was a boon to anyone fascinated by Vietnamese traditions, but I wished I'd come in low season when I found myself enmeshed in a sea of motorbikes crossing the city's broad boulevards. Inching through a seemingly impassible maelstrom of motorists, like a school of fish with fire-hot exhaust pipes, was not the most welcoming introduction to Ho Chi Minh City. Needless to say, every person in southern Vietnam seemed to be in the city then.

I crashed at a place offering a $5/night room in Pham Ngu Lao. It was so cozy that I could touch the walls on either side of my bed at the same time.

In several days I tired of the hustle of Ho Chi Minh City and cast my eyes on the long coast leading to Hanoi, where I had a general plan of staying for a while. I blazed through the quaint coastal town of Mui Ne, spending a night in a youth hostel after a trek through town and some red snapper on the beach that I picked out of the tank myself.

My wanderings delivered me next to the former holiday refuge of the French colonials, Da Lat. The nearly alpine environment of that small settlement was what originally drew the Europeans to build vacation homes there, and it still has a feeling of being far removed from the jungles, tropical coasts, and chaotic cities of the rest of the country.

Da Lat is famous foremost for the strawberries, flowers, and other delectables that fill its vast sweeps of nurseries and sloping ridges. It is called "Le petit Paris,"and there is even a miniature Eiffel Tower there. Despite these attempts by the French to imprint upon it their own character, it has much of its own originality that attracted me.

One example is the Crazy House, a seemingly Alice in Wonderland-inspired array of rooms rising like a surreal dream out of the ground. Technically a guesthouse, it's like a fairy tale on mescaline, a twisting and surprising trip of childhood fancy and playful anomaly.

Passing through the relatively uninteresting beach party of Nha Trang, I arrived in Hoi An, the entire old section of which is a UNESCO world heritage site. The architecture of the tiny winding streets has been magnificently preserved to appear as it did long ago, and is one of the most historical destinations in Southeast Asia.

After several days in Hue, the old imperial capital, I finally made it to Hanoi, a place that for years I had held as mythical, where it was my will to stay for a long time.

I arrived on an overcast morning after being up all night on the bus from Hue. Knowing nothing about the city's geography other than that Hoan Kiem was the area I wanted to be in, I ended up walking for miles all over the city that first day, falling in love with it.

I was attracted to Hanoi like it was a living being, more so than any other place I had ever been. It was very seductive, in the facades on houses, the old men with painter's hats bicycling down the street, and the grey cobblestone underneath. It felt very respectable, refined, yet enigmatic, enshrouded. There was a curious dichotomy to it. On the one hand there was the serenity of the lakes and parks, and on the other, the blitzkrieg whirlwind of people and motorbikes in the street. There was a palpable sense of reverence to history there. Under the shadow of glass and concrete high rises, on streets lit by neon, an ancient stillness refused to be edged away by the impulses of modernity.

I was swooned by its vibrancy. Out of such a turbulent past there seemed to be an immediacy, a poetic urgency to make a future capable of stability. I found the images I saw walking around to be intensely captivating and beautiful. Trees wildly draped themselves over rainy streets and fog hung in the air into midday. At Hoan Kiem lake, old people did tai chi, young lovers embraced surreptitiously, and others sat alone in the stillness that emanates from that mythic water.

I knew only the simple, everyday necessities of the language, but these coupled with a modicum of politeness rendered more toothy grins and warm handshakes than anywhere I had ever been. People are nice in their own way everywhere, but in Hanoi I found some of the most straightforward and hospitable people I have encountered anywhere.

Walking down the street in Hanoi was like a military exercise. With every step one has to guard against getting creamed by a motorbike, stepping on a family of chickens or an old woman's foot, knocking over a cigarette vendor's stock, falling into a hole in the ground, obstructing the path of a woman carrying baskets bulging with fruit, falling over a steaming cauldron of pho broth, or, dazed by these perpetual precautions, just slipping and falling the way one does in the course of a normal walk.

There was an unexpected fluidity to the chaos in the streets, and after a while I realized it wasn't chaos, but a seamless order. When crossing the street, the best thing to do, I found, was to just walk right across as if it were empty. The barrage of motorists would zip effortlessly around like the water in a river around a stone. It's a kind of order, a symbiotic disharmony that was remarkable to witness.

One day I was walking around Hoan Kiem, trying to find a way to rent an apartment for the next several months. I had just been hired at an English school for university students which paid my daily budget in an hour's work, and I needed to find something long term.

I happened across a message board near St. Joseph's cathedral with a flyer advertising apartments for foreigners. Calling the number, a guy answered and I asked about the apartments.

He said "yeah, I'm here," to which I responded, "what part of town?"

"I'm here, bro!"

"I know, I understand, *where*?"

He said it one more time but I realized his voice was coming from right behind me. I turned around and saw a young guy, about my age, dressed in a black and white suit with white leather shoes and a white belt.

"You looking for an apartment?"

"Yeah, I want to stay in Hanoi for six months, maybe longer."

"Ok, come inside my bar, we can talk."

His bar was right behind him and we stepped inside.

"My name's Lucky," he said, yanking the cap off of a bottle of beer.

"Many foreigners come here so I practice English every night. British, American, German. Many people."

"Nice to meet you, my name's Ian."

"Where you from?"

I have been fairly sensitive to my country's dealing with the world since I was a young adult, and I really didn't like saying I was an American while traveling. This was especially the case in Vietnam. The last thing I wanted was to have the question of 'I wonder if my dad killed your dad?' lingering about a casual conversation. A lot of times I would say I was from Norway.

But this time, I knew he would know, so I told the truth.

He said "ok, welcome to Hanoi, bro" and shook my hand before we got on to brass tacks about the apartment.

I liked Lucky from the start. He seemed like a straight up guy who genuinely wanted to help people out who were new to this seemingly unnavigable city. I would learn that was a strain of a very real kind of indigenous Vietnamese pride; infinitely agreeable to the foreign, ruthlessly averse to foreign rule. After a couple of beers we drove around the city on his motorbike, and I realized he didn't really have as much of a plan as I had assumed. We went from place to place, and many of them were so disgusting that even I politely refused to rent them.

Finally we made our way through a labyrinth of back streets in Hai ba Trung to a surprisingly swanky place. It was clean, had a full kitchen (sink, fridge, and range), a living room with flat screen TV, two bedrooms, two bathrooms, and a rooftop. Of course, all of this was crammed into a very small space, but it was much more than I needed.

"Oh this is super nice but way too big," I said. "I really just need a room with a toilet and a window."

"Maybe you can share it?" Lucky was playing with his phone and chatting in a very business-like way to the woman who owned it.

"I don't know anyone here, man. Not possible for a little while."

He coolly motioned for me to chill and hand him a lighter, putting his phone to his head and a cigarette in his mouth. After several minutes on the phone, he turned to me and said "my fay ontz and her friend also need a new place. Do you want to meet them?"

"Your what?"

"My fay ontz, fee ontz...how do you say it? My girlfriend but we are going to get married."

"Ahhh ok--- your fee ontz ay," I exclaimed, feeling like a dolt.

"Yeah...fee ontz ay...so is it ok?"

"Sure."

"Ok. We'll go back to the bar to talk to them. I'm sure it will be cool."

I thought it was kind of strange, to be honest, that we had just met that day and he was organizing for me to live in the same apartment as his fiance and her friend, but he didn't find it so and there was nothing to argue about.

We raced back to the bar. Why everyone was in such a goddamn hurry in Vietnam I couldn't understand. They could sit around lazily for hours smoking and drinking tea but when it was time to get on a motorbike you'd better hold onto your face.

We got to the bar and Lucky's fiance, Mai, and her friend, Vung, were already there. They were nice and evidently open to the idea of living with a complete stranger from the other side of the planet. If anything, I was taken aback and had to decide to just have faith in the situation, as what I cherished then most was my alone time when I was at home. I tended to do a lot of pacing and making cocktails, traits I didn't see myself able to do as flagrantly as I liked in this potential domicile. But, the place was cleaner and better positioned than I had planned on, and agreed with my budget.

With less aplomb or social formality than I was expecting, we rode back with them to their current place and helped them pack up what would be a Sisyphean amount for two motorbikes in any other country. After an hour or so of sitting around on the floor of the living room with the entire extended family of the owner, we signed some papers, got the keys, and our new landlord's clan slowly filtered out.

Lucky hung around for a little bit while the girls got all their things unpacked and set up. I put a couple of books and my clothes on the coffee table in my room, trying to make it feel a little more permanent, and we shot the breeze until he headed back to the bar.

At first I gave Mai and Vung a pretty wide berth, but after several days I realized that they were more comfortable living with me than I was with them, and we settled into a friendly routine. It was incredibly easy living with them. They were some of the best housemates I've ever had. They were from south of Hanoi by several hundred kilometers and told me all about their families, how they grew up, the things they loved and hated about Vietnam, and most of all, places they wanted to travel to. I had more fun sitting around on the living room floor with them, eating mangoes and sunflower seeds, watching movies on HBO with Vietnamese subtitles, than I would have had in a hundred years at corny expat bars.

I was able to photocopy entire English textbooks for next to nothing, and every day they would do a new unit in the books, which I would check at night while we were hanging out. Lucky would come over and the four of us would hunch over our books, they with the English courses and me with translations of Ho Chi Minh's poetry, while cheesy romantic comedies played on the TV. They were very astute and wanted to know every correct form of every verb and tense, and were in turn immensely helpful with my learning as much Vietnamese as I could. They were delightful times.

Chapter 11

In Hanoi my fortunes improved and I began to experience some stability. I had desired to stay there and set up camp for a while. In finding that job and the apartment with Mai and Vung, my plans were coalescing quite nicely. I would sit facing the small window in my room, drinking cup after cup of green tea and reading about Vietnamese history and culture. I had also begun meditating with regularity, as well as doing more visualization exercises. With some self-control I had weaned myself down to drinking only after the sun went down, and no more liquor. Only beer. My stomach hadn't given me any trouble since Siem Reap, and I wanted to get my nervous system back to somewhere within the range of human normalcy.

The routine that I would do once a day and sometimes twice, was three or four asanas of Hatha Yoga, without which I couldn't have leapt and shimmied through Hanoi with the ease that I did. After that I would do ten minutes of pranayama, a method of breath control whereby all manner of wonderful things happen, the first of which for me was the feeling that my lung capacity had expanded to far better than it had ever been. After regular practice of this, I could have run up and down the stairs as much as I wanted without getting short of breath. It also made the inside of my body feel cleaner.

I would sit in a chair in front of a timepiece that had a second hand. The way that I had learned to do it back when I lived in Portland was to inhale for ten seconds through one nostril, then plug it and exhale out the other for twenty. Then, inhale for ten seconds through the one I just exhaled through, switch, and exhale out the other for twenty. It takes some time to get into the rhythm of it, and can be exhausting at first, but after you get used to it, it's one of the most powerful and positive exercises ever conceived.

After pranayama, I would sit for ten minutes of meditation. I saw the value of meditation as being to cultivate a sense of control over the frenetic insanity of my mind. There are a million different ways and means of engaging a meditation practice, but I would sit and try to focus on an image to the point that I could hold it in my mind's eye for longer and longer periods of time. Doing this for ten seconds is far more difficult than it seems, and when one begins this practice, it is remarkable how easy we can be distracted from this ostensibly simple task by seemingly nothing at all.

After practicing with images in the mind, I would also experiment with sounds, smells, tastes, and tactile sensations, then combinations of them. With persistence, you can get to the point where your ability to imagine a situation is not too fundamentally different from actually experiencing it, and using this function to transform your life is the basis of what has been called magic, among other things, since ancient times.

The imaging part of the mind, the imagination, has many curious properties, and may or may not have the ability to affect the things that happen outside of it, in 'real life.' The idea that it does has been proposed by mystics, seers, and geniuses throughout history. It's not as if we can manifest our reality with a simple exercise, but if we strengthen our ability to imagine, I believe that we strengthen our ability to create. And, life is really one long creative process, however boring or beautiful its product is.

In a sense, we are what we think about. We are our habits. And during this time in Hanoi things were starting to converge within me that I felt were contributing to a more stable outlook on life. Many of the inessentials had been dissolved in the past several years. I had stripped away the clutter from my life. Now I was in a position to reform and rebuild my worldview, and my daily practice of life itself. These were aspects of the *coagula* in that alchemical equation.

I wouldn't consider the kinds of practices I was doing to be spiritual *per se*, although they could be called that. Essentially, they were techniques of mind management. Doing physical yoga definitely helps the body attain a sense of limberness and ease of activity, and meditation does the same for the mind. There doesn't need to be anything spiritual about that. No belief comes into the equation, only practicing techniques, to see if they work. This is the scientific method.

It became a very comforting thing for me to have these practices in my life. A daily practice like this becomes like a friend, a living being that you can look forward to seeing every day. The tumult caused by getting trashed early in the day was gone from my life, and I had a phenomenal amount of energy.

Everything was coming together, and it felt good. I was making it happen.

A humbling was not far into the future, however. One night, the police were making a check around to our place as they had doubtless learned of my presence in the labyrinthine alley where twenty families were stacked like cordwood. Mai and Vung were obviously angry at the officer's prodding, and didn't display the kind of politeness towards him one would expect.

However, upon scrutiny of my visa, he told me that he would be taking my passport and that I should visit the neighborhood police station in the morning. After balking and assuming he was surely mistaken, Mai and Vung listened to him explain that I had overstayed my visa by seventeen days. He showed us that '2/2/2010 – 5/3/2010' did not mean three months and one day, but one month and three days.

I had sworn I'd paid for three months at the embassy in Phnom Penh, and after my adrenaline subsided, I realize the egg was all over my face for making this stupid, obvious mistake. No one in Asia writes the month first like that. In my lack of discretion I had been rolling around Vietnam with an outdated visa for two and a half weeks, and there would surely be consequences I couldn't afford.

They tried to do what they could to talk to the officer, but he wasn't having any of it until the next morning when I was to come in and meet with immigration. He left and a pall cast itself over the apartment. We really had a good thing there, the three of us, and no one needed this hiccup.

I saturated myself in alcohol humorlessly in front of a *Rocky* marathon on HBO until I was passed out on the tile floor. I was planning on deportation, after perhaps several days in jail, just so they could prove their point.

As it turned out, I didn't have to go to jail or get deported, which was the fate of another young American guy who was also waiting at immigration. I assumed that had something to do with the fact that he had no shoes, and said he ate "when people give me food," and slept in the park. I ended up buying him a bowl of pho that evening, and he actually asked if they had vegetarian broth.

I had to pay an absolutely mental fine. $500. That was a fortune to me then. They had me by the balls, though, and there was nothing I could do but pay and whimper off. They added a three day extension from that day, giving me time to get somewhere, presumably Laos, to renew it should I decide to return.

Then there was the issue of my apartment. When I got back home that evening, Mai and Vung were not in their usual, chipper spirits. They said we couldn't stay. I had too many questions they couldn't answer in English so they called Lucky and gave me the phone. It turned out that the owner of the place got whacked by the police, as well. You have to have some sort of license to rent to foreigners, and he hadn't gone through this formality.

As a result, he supposedly had to pay a large fine. Since I had only lived there for about two weeks and had paid for three months up front, the damning reality I divined from this, confirmed by Lucky, was that I was out my two and a half months' rent, another mammoth amount of cash to me at the time. My daily budget for food was $5. I couldn't afford to lose that money, but it was not up to me, and Lucky even came to talk to the guy.

We sat on his floor with his family for a very uncomfortable hour but he basically told us to piss off. I felt bad asking for the money back, sitting on the concrete floor with his whole family, but I had tried to ensure that we wouldn't have to deal with this problem when I moved in. I guess he hadn't been completely up front with us.

I felt like a complete asshole. This debacle had cost me about two months of living expenses. Small beans in the grand scheme, no doubt, but at the time it was pretty gutting. I was way down on funds, would have to find another place, and Mai and Vung would have to, as well. My resolve had taken a beating. I wasn't snapping back into form the way I wished and expected myself to.

The wind was really knocked out of my sails. Sitting in the internet shop amongst teenagers playing video games and yelling at each other, I longed for everything to just be simple. I wanted to surround myself with simple, meaningful things. I wanted to escape the carnal din of the city and watch the grass grow.

I was going to have to go to Laos to get my new Vietnamese visa, so I decided to just stay there. Fuck finding another apartment, fuck the insanity of the city, and fuck bars full of women who would never interest me.

I wanted to live on a farm. Learn some new things. Watch the weather change.

I looked on the internet to see if there were any farms where I could work in Laos and found the Vang Vieng Organic Farm. I wrote down the directions and was on a bus to Vientiane that afternoon.

Chapter 12

The bus ride from Hanoi to Vientiane took around twenty six hours, and I was beating the shit out of myself the whole time.

Arriving at the center of town from the bus station by tuk tuk, I was surprised to see how small Vientiane was. I kept thinking that the rest of the city had to be stashed somewhere else.

The cheapest guesthouse I could find off of the Mekong River was $5 a night, the walls plastered with signs explaining that Laotian women were not allowed entry with guests. I dropped the unimportant things from my bag on the bunk, doused my face and hair with cold water, and headed out to explore postage-stamp sized Vientiane.

After seeing most of the larger streets and waltzing through a few temples, I found myself back at the river approaching a convenience store with tables and chairs, and decided to get a beverage. I picked up a bottle of Tiger Whisky for a dollar, as well as a can of soda, a plastic cup, and sat down on the patio. After making myself a drink I sat and looked out at the river, dazed and loaded with uncertainty. A guy with piercing blue eyes was watching me, grinning.

After several minutes, he said "hey buddy."

"Hey."

"You smoke?" I was already smoking a cigarette.

"Yeah," I said, waving the cigarette in the air to reiterate.

"No. Do you smoke?"

"Ah." I moved over to his table.

"Look at this." He opened his cigarette pack and showed me a handful of joints that looked like they'd been rolled by a machine.

"Listen, I'm not looking to get into any shit, man."

"Do I look like a fucking Laotian cop, man?"

He was still grinning.

We got up and walked across the street to the promenade beside the river, and descended halfway down the concrete steps on the bank and sat down. He pulled out a joint and lit it up without looking around, or any conspicuousness in the broad daylight. Taking a few puffs, he handed it over.

"Mo."

"I'm sorry?"

"My name's Mo." I couldn't place his accent.

"I'm Ian." I shook his hand. He was gazing across the river, his head tilted lazily to the side.

"You know what is over there?"

"No, what?"

"Thailand."

"Really? Right there?" I hadn't realized the border was that close.

"Right there, man." He wasn't grinning so much anymore, but smiling as if cherishing memories much further away than the swaying trees on the other side of the Mekong.

"I had a life there. I had wife. I had business. Import, export."

I nodded and passed him the joint.

He looked at it with nostalgia and raised it to his lips.

"I had many years there. Many very happy years. My wife, she is still there. But she is not my wife anymore." A fisherman was rowing his boat out to the middle of the river.

"She stays there now, for a long time. They are the bittersweet memories. Every day I come here and look over at her."

After several months in Vietnam without smoking, whatever was rolled up in that joint was getting right up on top of me.

"What happened?"

"Ah. She got away. You know? I am not Thai and...there was problem. Her brothers, they don't like me."

"Where are you from?"

"Lebanon" he said, perking up and glancing at me, grinning again. He seemed happy to change the subject.

"And you?"

"The States."

I was starting to get tunnel vision, with alternating cold and hot waves throughout my body, and felt myself becoming one with the concrete we were sitting on. I struggled to move the bottle of whiskey away from my feet in fear I would knock it over.

"Are you Christian?"

The colors drained out of my view of the river and everything was an amalgam of fuzzy grays and sepias. My hands and feet were going numb and I moved my hands around on my lap to see if I could feel anything.

"No, I don't consider myself Christian, although I was raised Christian."

"You have no religion?"

"I think that...all religions have truth. Muslim, Christian, Buddhist, Hindu, whatever. They are like...so many poems about the same sunset."

I touched my face and hair, and moved my feet around underneath me. It was as if they were suspended in water.

"I am a Muslim." He passed me the joint.

"No, no, thank you. Jesus what is that? Normal weed? I think I'm going blind..."

He grinned and continued smoking.

"We are from the same book, same God, you and I."

"Yeah, yeah...."

I was having a hard time just sitting upright and breathing. I put my head between my knees and tried to breathe deep breaths. It was embarrassing.

"People of the book."

"Yes, people of the book. Although I'm not Christian..."

"The Quran is a very beautiful book. And poetry. The most beautiful in the world."

"I've heard that."

"You know the story of Ishmael?" He put the joint out under his shoe.

My interest was piqued.

"Abraham's son...with Hagar? Abraham's maid or something? They went off away from Abraham and Sarah, and Ishmael was the...father of the Arabs?"

"Yes, precisely. Do you know what then happened?"

He continued, telling me that story, and then many other stories from the Quran, the selection of which had to have been the most bizarre in the whole book. I had grown up reading the Old Testament, so holy book weirdness was something I was well accustomed to, but these were all new to me.

Soon he was standing and gesticulating, I his obliging audience, genuinely interested in this bardic session, but unable to control my motor functions. I was swaying back and forth like those inflated men they put in front of used car dealerships, too high to respond to anything beyond occasionally making eye contact and saying "oh yeah?"

Pretty soon he suggested we go eat something.

"You don't look so good."

"I need to eat something."

"OK let's go." He waved his hand and was off, and I staggered to my feet and stumbled after him, blindly following towards the road. We got to a Mexican restaurant and shimmied up to the bar, ordering a couple of Beerlaos,

"I think I need to take a little nap" I slurred, trying to stay on the stool.

"Yeah man, you're fucked up."

"Just an hour or two. I want to hang out, but...I haven't smoked...or slept...in a long time."

"Ok buddy. You come back here later. We need to hang out. You have a good mind."

"Definitely. Ok. Bye bye."

I put my bag on my back, carefully got down from the stool, and stumbled away towards my hotel, searching my pockets for the key. A couple of hours of sleep sounded like a delicious idea.

* * * * * * * * * *

Later that evening I woke up, feeling relatively normal again, and went down to explore Vientiane. I spent the evening between the Mexican bar, the Red Mekong, and sitting on the river bank smoking with Mo. It was a relief hanging out with him, talking about esoteric and arcane subjects, compared to a gaggle of western twenty somethings clucking about which dive resort they got their PADI at or which jungle treks they'd been on. He gave me a handful of joints when we parted ways at the end of the night. We wished each other luck and I went back to pass out again in the bunk.

Chapter 13

I got the first van heading north to Vang Vieng the next morning. I was thinking about everything Mo and I were talking about the night before.

Anthropologists have never discovered a group of people who did not have some kind of creation myth, cosmology, and explanation for our relationship with beings that allegedly put us here. Religion is as much a part of the experience of our species as is art, language, cooking, and structure building. It is essentially neutral. It can be used for purposes that are life-affirming *or* life-denying. And comparatively, religions are like languages. No one would posit that French is a more true, valid, or capable language than Basque, Russian, Japanese, or Sumerian. They each serve the communicative needs of their speakers. I saw the mosaic of the world's religions in the same light.

And I also saw the spiritual instinct as being an ingrown, human trait. We are spiritual beings just as we are physical, sexual, emotional, and intellectual beings.

By the time I was twenty or so, I was immersed in the study of not only the major religions of the world, but specifically their esoteric, or inner, mystical facets, the sides of those traditions which have usually been shunned by their exoteric, or outer forms. Like Qabala in Judaism, Christian mysticism,

Sufism in Islam, and the vast corpus of the Western esoteric tradition such as Astrology, Tarot, Magic, and Alchemy. This relationship between the exoteric and the esoteric, similar to that between the orthodox and the heterodox, is one of the most dynamic and powerful in human history. In most major traditions, from Jesus, Buddha, Mohamad, Lao Tzu, and so on, you will find at the core a mystical experience, a revelation. That is the realm of the esoteric. What comes after, the dogma and clergy, is the exoteric. It's important to see the difference. There have always been mystical, occult traditions which have suffered at the hands of the priest classes, the wielders of empty dogma, and the masses which cling to and perpetuate their authority. If Jesus were around to see some of the sociopaths who invoke his name today, he wouldn't be able to stop puking.

There is no doubt that religion has been responsible for countless egregious things in history. And many of those things were also due to the banality of power systems and authoritarian control, yet took the form of religiosity for self-justification. For instance, when the Spanish and Portuguese came to the Americas, they may have come under the banner of Christianity, but its obvious that the reason they came was to take gold back home. That has nothing to do with religion.

In categorically condemning religion, there is the danger of throwing out the baby with the bathwater. Being wise means separating the wheat from the chaff, not burning the field down.

Either way, the conviction I had was that each of us has a kind of vehicle by which we can experience the numinous, the transcendent, the universal, what many throughout history have called the Spirit. That vehicle is unique to each person, and it can be accessed and expressed in whatever way our proclivities advance. It is our connection, our umbilical cord to the infinite. We can call it a spirit or a soul or whatever we like. It doesn't really matter. It's there within each of us, waiting to be unfolded like a rose.

As the bus lumbered to a stop under the beating sun, I remembered the words of Christ in the Gospel of Luke..."the kingdom of heaven is within you..."

After picking up a bottle of water and a bag of peanuts, I sauntered into the road to see about the location of the farm. I approached a woman with her back to me and said hello, watching her scoop a bucket of water out of a large drum. She then proceeded to turn around and gracefully, reverently, pour it all over my head and shoulders.

After a very confused moment, she explained to me that it was the first day of the Lao New Year. During these three days, in a blitzkrieg attack with buckets, water pistols, and hoses of water on any and everyone, the rainy season would be ritually ushered in, and a new, plentiful, prosperous year in its stead. This is celebrated, in many parts of Laos, Cambodia, and Thailand, by the ritual drenching of everyone in sight.

She informed me that the farm was a couple kilometers north, and I began walking to my destination.

There were many people in front of shops and houses with buckets and water guns, I tried to make it apparent that I had just got off a bus, had all my stuff on me, and that it wouldn't be the most felicitous of gestures for me to be drenched again. This would change by the next day, when I would take part in the most outrageously fun, raucous, life-affirming public celebration I had ever seen, in a cacophonous deluge of water, cornmeal, dye, and ash.

The main attraction of Vang Vieng for young Western tourists was to get heroically shit-faced and float along the idyllic Nam Song river, serenaded by house remixes of "Don't Stop Believing" and "Roxanne". Some of the more courageous and socially desperate of the flotilla would enamor fellow tubers with quixotic attempts to jump off of shoddy structures into areas of dubious depth. Young Laotian boys snorkeled there in the mornings, retrieving wallets and passports sealed in water tight bags dropped by their owners the day before.

Bank-side watering holes offering Beerlao and free shots of Tiger whiskey accompany the trip. It's an embarrassing sight to behold bikini-clad women staggering about, looking for a place to vomit while a group of young monks shuffle around them to get to the path leading to their temple.

I hitched a ride on the back of a truck for the remaining kilometer of the journey and was dropped off at the entrance to the farm on a gravel road just off the main road. There was a restaurant with many people milling about, and I went to the counter to get a beer and find a room. It was an already friendly price, which would drop precipitously with all the time I spent working on the farm.

I got my key and the woman pointed me in the right direction. Walking past frolicking dogs and Mulberry, Lime, Kiwi, and Papaya trees, a family of geese waddled to the side of the trail that lead to the dormitory. I hauled up the steps to the front porch area which had entrances to several private rooms, and the dorm. The door was open, and there were several people sitting in beds chatting, reading, and dozing. A bed at the end was empty so I flopped my bag on it and said 'hello.'

There was a large family who owned and lived on the farm, and several Laotian agricultural students from Vientiane doing an internship who also lived there. Staying in the dorm and the various other rooms, some of which were mud houses, was an assortment of other travelers keen to know more about organic farming and sustainable living. There was a young dreaded guy from Melbourne who was planning on starting an urban farm back home, a girl from Philadelphia who had been tattooing people in Bangkok for a long time but was out of Thailand for some visa reasons, a young Canadian college student on a summer trip, a Dutch veterinarian and animal rights activist, and Foukzy, a French guy who had spent a long time in Isaan doing Muay Thai training amongst many other places he'd been living in Southeast Asia.

After a fantastic evening drinking and playing songs on the guitar with the other people from the dorm, I woke up the next morning, besotted and beguiled, and walked down to the goat pens.

The basic schedule revolved around the tending of the goats, as well as working in the Mulberry fields and making cheese.

The first order of the day was to sweep the pens out, and then to change the water buckets. After some trepidation before going into the initial pen, imagining one of the horns going straight up my ass, I began sweeping and cooing the goat to serenity.

They're fascinating animals, something I had never realized from just seeing them on a screen or at a petting zoo as a child. They are curiously willful, which connotes intelligence, but they seem simultaneously confused, disturbed, and stupid. I resonated with them, and began to think about the symbolism they had provided to the world's mythological canon.

These adorable creatures have been much maligned in the Christian West, owing to a few historical accidents of ignorance.

The Knights Templar, the richest, most powerful and adept knights of the Crusades, unwittingly started some of this original goat fear. After confessing, under duress of torture, to a litany of heresies they may or may not have committed, one of the strangest was that they worshipped and consulted as an oracle a goat's head, which some called "Baphomet." There were several permutations of this legend, but the oracle was considered to be terrifying and all-knowing.

If we fast forward to the early nineteenth century, we find the classic image of Baphomet in the book Transcendental Magic by the French seminarian and occultist, Eliphas Levi. This image shows a creature with a goat's head and legs, wings, and a human torso with female breasts and a large caduceus or wand for a penis. On its forehead is a pentagram, and a torch burns from the top of its head. Its right arm is emblazoned with *solve* and its left arm with *coagula*, that axiom which had become so important to me on my birthday in Koh Tao.

This is the image which Christians, Satanists, and metal bands alike have attributed to Satan. Levi, who composed this image and codified our understanding of the symbolism of Baphomet, never says anything about Satan. To the contrary, Levi considered Baphomet to be a glyph of the union of all opposites, the rectification of the dichotomy of good and evil, and a kind of etheric agent of psychological evolution. It doesn't represent evil, or good, but deliverance from the antipathy of both, not too dissimilar to the symbol of yin-yang.

This all gave me much to meditate upon while kneeling and milking the goats in the mornings.

* * * * * * * * * * *

Foukzy and I bounced along the dirt path from the farm and up onto the main road. Trucks were driving past in both directions festooned with children and teenagers wielding water guns, buckets, and balloons. Each one would have its own large reserve of water for refilling. They were roving gangs of Buddhist blessing, the mirth radiant in front of every business and intersection.

The scenario we had planned out was that Foukzy would be the heroic driver and I would be the heroic gunman, taking out any potential risk that came within range of fire. The idea was to take them out first, momentarily blinded and unable to direct their buckets at us.

It was the most outrageously fun celebration of a holiday I have ever, and probably will ever, experience. Everyone was jubilant and laughing, usually freshly blasted and going for more water. Both of us were drenched from the first five minutes of heading out to arriving back at the farm late that evening.

We were hunting around trying to find every cave that we could in the amount of time we had the bike. Fighting our way through the gauntlet of the main road south through town, I tried to make my hits before we immediately sped through to miss each ensuing deluge.

Cruising through rice paddies and farms, around karsts and over rivers, we passed a wooden sign with the words "Blue Lagoon Cave" painted on it, and motored on in the direction of the arrow. Trying to divine the meaning of each crude sign that would follow, we eventually got to a clearing with a small refreshment stand. An old man was playing cards with a young boy.

"Sabai dee," we said and asked him about the cave. He pointed over in the direction of the base of a karst and said "Ok."

We followed along the path, putting on our headlamps. Foukzy said "have you ever been in a cave?"

"No. Have you?"

"A couple times, in France. But they were lit inside, and we had a guide. This is very different."

"Yeah. I'm shitting myself."

He laughed and we started in.

It was fairly straightforward for about ten meters until the light slowly faded out, our headlamps growing brighter in the darkness. We arrived at a large piece of rock that almost blocked the way we were walking. We could barely see that there was a half meter of sloping, wet mud to navigate around it.

You had to bear-hug the stone in order to not fall into an large opening in the ground beside it.

"Oh, fuck me," I muttered, thinking of heading back.

"That's a tricky one."

Foukzy picked up a small stone and tossed it into the hole which was big enough around for several people to fall in at once. At once cliche and terrifying, we didn't hear the stone hit anything after he tossed it in. I picked up another one and did the same. Still no sound.

"Well look; you can put your arms around it like this, and grab these spots, and keep as close to the stone as you can, and the ground is still level enough to get around without slipping. Watch."

He began to do exactly as he had explained, and made it over to the other side. I did the same, a chill going through the back of my legs as I glanced down at the blackness. If one fell in, it would be a very long time, if ever, before getting out.

"No problem!" Foukzy smiled and laughed. I was thinking about being mangled hundreds of feet down at the bottom.

We continued on, covered in clay and mud as we shimmied over and under the guts of the mountain. It was often a smaller space than we could stand in, and required constant vigilance against slipping, and being on the lookout for more gaping holes to fall in. Luckily there was really only one direction in which to proceed, which alleviated my concerns of getting lost.

I'd never heard that kind of silence before. Foukzy suggested we make plenty of noise so that snakes and other creatures would know well enough ahead of our approach to not be startled by us.

After a little while the walls around us spread out and the ceiling lifted to about ten meters, making the first large chamber we'd come across.

"Oh, wow Ian, look..."

Standing before us was a large statue of the Buddha, maybe five meters in height, smiling serenely down on the pitch blackness that surrounded him.

"How did they do that?"

"Amazing. They must have carved it in here."

We stood and rested in front of it for a few minutes. I needed a drink.

"Let's go a little further."

We continued out of the chamber with the statue and the space encroached around us again. It became a long, straight passageway, and the walls were covered in crystals. In spite of how diabolical the cave seemed to me, it was one of the most astoundingly beautiful things I'd ever seen. We stood and looked at the walls as they shimmered and seemed to move with our headlamps.

All of the sudden, immediately above and beside us, close enough to be on our skin, there was a howling, buzzing noise like a bullroarer.

"BZZZZZZZZZZZZZZZZZZZZZZZZZ"

"Oh my GOD!" I ducked and covered my head, and could see Foukzy in the strobing light of my headlamp trying cover his head.

"OUT! FINISHED!"

We crept and crawled along as quickly as we could without falling and knocking a skull or shin against jagged rock. I was sure that we would be eaten alive. The noise became less threatening as we moved away from it and we stopped to catch our breaths after arriving back within the chamber containing the Buddha statue, gasping in the seeming safety it radiated.

"What the hell was that?" I panted in a strained, terrified whisper.

"Ask the Buddha."

We both began laughing hysterically under the muted gaze of the statue, and decided we'd explored enough of that cave, heading back the way we came. When the light began to peek through, I thought how emerging from a cave had to be one of the most redeeming things a human could experience. I stepped out into the sun, stretching my hands up to the sky.

We drank a bottle of water and smoked a cigarette with the old man, who told us about the other caves in the area, some with gigantic caverns, some you had to crawl through, some you could swim deep down inside of in the pitch black. Bowing, thanking, and wishing him 'happy new year,' we got on the bike and ambled back through the dirt paths, trying to follow his directions to other caves.

We made it to two more, one which was the size of a cathedral inside, and felt very much like being on another planet. Another had incredibly clear water in a small lagoon, but when I waded in, about a hundred tiny fish immediately swam out to feast on the skin covering my feet and ankles. I scrambled up the rocks while Foukzy fell over himself with laughter.

While traveling between them we were getting soaked at every turn. Sometimes kids would run out from behind trees, too quick for me to pump the gun, leaving us with no defense. There were a few times when I hit some kids dead in the face, with maybe a little too much precision, but they took it all in stride, running after us, pitching water balloons and trying to make the best machine gunner stance.

One time, we were approaching a small wooden bridge with a handful of people gathered around, ready for our approach. A group of older women stood in our path. They congregated around us with buckets of water and slowly poured them over our heads and shoulders, smiling and speaking blessings, while others rubbed red pigments and perfumed talcum powder on our faces and arms.

It wasn't until the sun was setting that we made it back to the farm, our flesh pruned and chafed. I took a shower and sat on the porch of the dormitory, sipping a whiskey and water. Some of the others arrived, and we began to toss back and forth our stories of the insane party that was the Lao New Year.

All of the sudden, an older American guy ran up to the porch like his face was on fire.

"Hey everybody! You gotta get down there! They're killin' a goat!"

In unison, we rose with embarrassed, morbid curiosity.

Jogging down to a small clearing by the Mulberry field, we could see one of the farmers brandishing a blowtorch, going to town on the freshly-slit goat. Its body was expanded like a balloon, I supposed from all the heat of the flame.

"What's with the blowtorch?" I asked the American guy.

"Get all the hair off, I guess," he said, his wide eyes fastened to the sight.

The Laotians were happy we'd joined them. One of them had the knives, grinning from ear to ear, while several others stood around watching, hooting, and drinking whiskey Lao Lao. Evidently many goats had met their demise in that area because there were goat skulls hanging about on the trees.

"You know, this is really terrific? I've been looking all over for a place where I can have a black mass, as well as the right venue for my metal band. I can't believe my luck in finding this place!" I said, gesturing at the skulls. I thought that was pretty funny.

It made me feel like a real creature of the city to see an animal being butchered for the first time. The closest I'd been to this was a steak wrapped in bar-coded paper from the grocery store.

The shirtless, knife-wielding farmer seemed glad to have an audience of squeamish, captivated Westerners on hand for the occasion. He had obviously done this a thousand times, working with fluid precision. The organs were hauled out one by one, and the toxic guts were separated from the edibles. When he pulled the stomach out he held it triumphantly up to the rest of us, and stepped away from the tarp the goat was lying on before flashing a demonic grin and puncturing it. The contents spewed out in a repulsive torrent of green slime. The woman standing beside me turned away and covered her mouth.

One of the Laotians proudly handed me a plastic cup of whiskey Lao Lao. I have never hesitated so much before taking a drink, but I downed its vile, jet fuel tasting contents while watching the last of the goat's lunch drip out of the stomach. It was with Herculean resolve that I kept mine from doing the same.

The other farmers took the ribs and slid them in makeshift bamboo racks, rubbing them with some kind of spice and placing them over the fire. Everyone had a few rounds of whiskey and began to warm up to the occasion.

The ribs were plucked off the fire and pulled apart onto a plate, passed around to all of us. I picked one up and thanked the goat aloud before biting off a chunk of its brown, slightly charred flesh. It was juicy, surprisingly tender, slightly sweet, and delicious. Goat ribs became one of my favorite foods while standing there.

Soon the goat was unrecognizable and the usable parts were placed in a large tub for the women in the kitchen to go to work on for the evening's feast. The last of the plastic bottle of Lao Lao was finished and the skull was washed and reverently placed in its own special part of the tree containing the others. Some still in a mild shock from the gory spectacle, we filtered back to the porch after thanking the farmers profusely for sharing the goat's bounty.

I did my nightly English lesson with the restaurant staff and farmers, and had one of the most memorable meals of my life. After an incredible amount of food, I walked back to the dormitory full and festive, glad to be alive.

That night was spent like the others, drinking and singing songs with the guitar, and remembering the martyred animal.

＊ ＊ ＊ ＊ ＊ ＊ ＊ ＊ ＊ ＊

When I woke the next morning, I was in a private room, in bed with a Dutch woman who'd arrived the day before.

"Well, well, well! This is a nice surprise!"

She smiled, looking into my eyes.

"Why do you drink so much?"

It hit me like a cannonball. I began sobbing with my whole body. She had pulled a lynchpin. The levee broke. I laid there and cried without concerning myself that she could see me, that others might hear me. All of the failings I had carried with me, all of my remorse at letting myself become so ensnared in such a crippling addiction, and all of the sadness that inspired it, flowed through me. My aura shivered. She held my head as my body heaved with sobbing. I dammed myself up and robotically changed the subject. After a little while she got dressed and said "let's have some breakfast, shall we?"

I put on my sunglasses and walked with her down to the cafe overlooking the river, and we ate fresh baguettes with honey and goat cheese from the farm, talking about her trip from Vientiane to Kathmandu the next evening, and how excited she was to meet her grandfather there.

The topic of me drinking wasn't brought up again. I didn't want to talk to anyone about it. It pained me too much to consider how I hadn't the will or self-control to live even a single day without it. I pushed it back down and returned to the dorm to see what the others were up to.

I was at the farm a few more days before getting down to the last allowed by my visa. Wresting myself from its bucolic environs, I hitched up to Luang Prabang. I would spend my remaining three days there.

Luang Prabang is known as one of the most spiritual places in Southeast Asia. Many would say the world, and for good reason. There are Buddhist temples everywhere, and one of its most iconic images is the early morning procession of monks through the center of town to receive alms and rice from villagers, chanting hypnotic blessings upon them. It is these elements of the very traditional and very Buddhist Laotian culture which bring people to Luang Prabang, and however this may affect it in the future, its vibration must evoke appreciation from even the most foam-mouthed atheist. It is arrestingly peaceful, and the prospect of healing, in whatever way or form, is palpable in the air.

However, for me, this sentiment remained little more than a nice idea. I slept on the front steps of a different temple every night, waking up in the early morning with a scattering of dogs and usually a small cushion someone had laid beside my head during the night. Of my internal state at the time, I remember a sadness of desert proportion that the people I loved the most couldn't share this place and time with me. There was an intoxicated sense of fading away, yet I felt infinitely blessed for having been able to know and appreciate such a remarkably special place on the planet.

I was living in a kind of bizarre, liminal state, almost between the living and the dead. The arrestingly sublime beauty of Vang Vieng and Luang Prabang were juxtaposed by the intractable knowledge that returning to America might be a reality if I didn't find a job somewhere fast. I woke up one morning with the dogs at a temple, made sure I had everything on me, and went to find the first ticket I could to Thailand. It was the last day of my Lao visa.

There was a bus in a few hours to Chiang Rai. I would have a couple more weeks, up in the Golden Triangle, to figure out how the hell this plane was possibly going to land.

Chapter 14

At the farm in Vang Vieng, I had experienced a true idyll. The bed in which I slept and the food I ate were provided by my labor. The only money I had to spend was on the occasional dollar bottle of Tiger Whiskey and ten cent packs of cigarettes. I would walk amongst the papaya and lime trees in the moonlight, utterly content. Content to sit in the evenings on the porch and rest my eyes on that invigoratingly beautiful landscape, perforated by majestic, mist-enshrouded, limestone karsts, stunningly green mountains, and the most kind people I had ever spent time with.

I had left Laos because my visa was up and I had to go to Thailand to renew it, but I was starting to come out of that paradisiacal haze and realize some brass tacks of the situation. I didn't have enough cash to keep doing this. I'd spent most of what I'd brought with me, and the money I'd made in Hanoi was eaten up entirely by the fines and lost rent owed to the visa debacle. I wasn't too sure what my options were. I had a vague notion that I could get a job in Thailand, but it was murky. I couldn't go back to Korea to teach because their visa restrictions were tighter now, and my prior disorderly conduct misdemeanor from years ago would now prohibit my employ in that country.

I knew fundamentally that I wouldn't be able to return and live in the States. I didn't even really have a home there. My friends were all over the world at that point. I could go back to Portland, but the last time I was there the only job I could find was the graveyard shift at a convenience store. I remembered that vividly. One night a guy tried to purchase alcohol after two am, and when I politely refused to sell it to him, owing to the law, he promised to come back and sodomize me with a florescent light. Charming place.

I could go back to Taos, but I was sure it'd be just as hard to find a job there as well. The situation in the States was downright bleak. No one could find any work, and it was astronomically expensive to live there, especially compared with how I'd been living for several years in Asia. Besides, the States was full of violent crime, the worst kind of drugs, and the values and morals of the place, in practice, were way out of my comfort zone at that point. I felt much more at home in the intensely conservative Buddhist countries I'd been living than I ever would in the States.

It's not that I didn't love it, in my own way. If curiosity and the desire to know about a place convey love or appreciation of it, then I loved the U.S. I had driven across it seven or eight times. I had lived all over the place, in Taos, Portland, Burlington and Boston, after having been raised in Kansas. Mine was not merely an empty, rhetorical, blind, unexamined love of the States, but a lustful, rich, experiential, deeply inquisitive love.

Consequently, my hatred of things about the U.S. was equally well-rooted. I've never been to a country with so many rules, regulations, and barriers to basic freedom. You have to show your government issued ID to buy a pack of cigarettes there. That's absolutely insane. And this, among countless of these instances, in a country that never tires of beating its chest about how it is the primary harbinger of freedom in the world!

The amount of sterility, uniformity, and paranoia in that place tower over any other that I've been to. The loudest and most apparent freedom most Americans have is that of being able to choose between Colgate or Crest, which are actually owned by the same company. This is a damning analog to the choice they make at the voting booths.

There is a nationalistic fervor in the U.S. that is almost religious, and that in the worst way possible. Many Americans have a kind of mythical reverence for their country, and react hysterically to any intimation that American forces have committed grave, systematic injustices in the world. There is an abysmal amount of disconnect from reality resultant from this pseudo-religious fervor. There are suburban evangelicals who actually believe that they and Benjamin Franklin would share the same worldview. There are actually people, many of them, who believe that Ho Chi Minh's independence movement, the Iraqi National Guard, and the Nicaraguan Sandinistas actually posed a threat to the security of the United States.

It is not a Christian country, and it never has been. If it were, they'd be spending trillions on food, medicine, and schools for the poor of the world, instead of cruise missiles, fighter jets, and aerial drones. I grew up reading the words of Christ telling us we should love our neighbors as ourselves, that peacemakers are blessed, that we should turn the other cheek when others wrong us. These sentiments are diametrically opposed to the endeavors of U.S. foreign policy since the Spanish-American War. As Wilhelm Reich said, "the ocean of lies in this world is deep."

No doubt there are incomparably incredible things that are the product of American genius, like the light bulb, the telephone, the airplane, the computer, the internet, and The Ramones. But none of these make more rosy the consequences of the U.S.' legion military exploits abroad since World War II.

No, I didn't want to go back. I knew that.

During the past several years of my life, there'd been an insane amount of romping, stumbling, and staggering, and as long as I could remember, there was always a drive to reach out, go further, and get weirder. And, I'd always had an unshakeable conviction that there was some kind of psycho-spiritual destination to our lives, that there was some kind of inner process we must each uniquely go through to reach a kind of inner paradise, if you will.

Perhaps it sounded grandiose when I had stated on my birthday in Koh Tao that I wanted to find the path of the hero, but that was what I saw as the whole point of life, in my clumsy, mislaid way. I had thought, hoped, wished, surmised, and demanded that my life should have a path, a purpose, a plot. It must be there. There must be some kind of answer to the riddle of my existence.

I believed that it was a waste of time looking for the hero externally, on screens and in stories. The real hero was us, our lives, our psyches, our souls. Beset by a million choices, chances, triumphs, and tragedies, I was navigating through the vicissitudes of life and had to somehow find the plot.

In the stories we have told ourselves throughout history, around campfires and coffee tables, there is the integral desire to seek some kind of gold at the base of our being. Rescuing damsels in distress, slaying dragons, and aspiring to thrones are really all symbolic of inner, psycho-spiritual processes.

I thought that the way to understand the path of the hero was by first doing the work of figuring out what my innermost nature was. My belief was that each of us, like a celestial body, have our own unique orbit, trajectory, and velocity, that each of us have a reason for being here, that the purpose of this experience on the planet Earth is to find it and do it, with all the courage, finesse, dedication and passion that we all undoubtedly somehow possess. This might be in biochemistry, poetry, house building, footballing, or cooking. That is up to each individual to seek, behold, and bear out in the way that only they can. The only sin in my worldview was trying to force one's will upon another. Besides, if you are doing that, then you aren't really doing your own.

Sometimes we need to vacillate, to stumble, to stagger around until we are led to it, perhaps by a kind of inner divination. However, I had no idea where the fuck I was going. I didn't know what was in my future. When I looked into my mind's crystal ball and attempted to divine an image of the future, it was like a black hole. I definitely could not see myself with a mortgage, a car payment, a stable career, a wife, kids. None of that.

The alcohol didn't help my worldview much, either. I became fatalistic. Far from providing a refuge from my existential dilemmas, it made things worse. It became easier to assume more and more that I was at the end of something, that this show was almost over. It became easier, going from bottle to bottle, stewing in *weltschmerz*, to develop an attitude that maybe it was time to just push the reset button.

I began to think how easy it would be to just go to sleep forever. I could just eat a bunch of pills. People did it all the time. People died every nanosecond.

Though it was extremely unsettled, it was not a dark time. I had had a rich life. I was happy with my life. I had the kind of friends I wanted, I had the kind of experiences I wanted, I had seen a lot of the kinds of places I wanted to see. But, there was nothing to snap out of, no phase to be wrested from. I wasn't going to change. Neither was the world around me. I wasn't going to wake up in some kind of utopia governed by ascended masters, where racism, war, sexism, homophobia, violence, and coercion were purged from the human experience.

My head was heavy with this mess as I woke around eight to go find some refreshments. There was a bar down the street, which to my delight had a TV with BBC on. When I walked up it was quite full, and the only seat open was in a booth across from an older guy, sitting in front of a Heineken, intently watching the news.

I asked if he minded me sitting across the booth. He shook his head and moved his things closer to his half of the table, taking little notice of me. I flagged the waitress down, ordering a bottle of water, a bottle of tomato juice, and a coke with ice.

I had the remains of a bottle of Sang Som in my bag with which I could make my own drink. One of the nice things about those parts of the world was that no one seemed to care if you brought your own booze, provided you were surreptitious about it, and you didn't see them see you doing it.

She brought the beverages and I drank down the water and the tomato juice. I pulled the rum from my bag, and poured a few fingers over the ice, filling up the little space left in the glass with coke.

"Good idea."

He was British, probably in his early sixties, and looked like he drank as much as I did.

"Well, one does what's necessary. You have to be crafty if you need to make it last."

"And don't I know it...I'm going broke with these imports, but I can't drink any more piss-tasting Thai beer."

"And you don't think Heineken tastes like piss?"

"Well, maybe the bottle has some kind of effect."

We drank for several minutes and watched the headlines flash across the bottom of the screen.

"How do you like this place?"

"What, Chiang Rai?" he said, finishing his beer off while motioning to the waitress for another.

"Yeah."

"It's a strange place. Full of freaks. Half these guys"

He lowered his voice.

"half these guys you see walking around are under the hammer. This is the golden triangle, dude. Loads of junkies and crazy ex-intelligence guys. Not the best vibe."

He smiled at his beer and clinked his rings against the bottle.

"Well why are you here, then?"

"Just to drop in on some old friends."

He winked as the waitress sat another Heineken in front of him.

He said "what about you?" turning away from the TV to face me.

"Oh, it's alright, I guess. I don't really know what I'm doing here. My visa was up in Laos so I'm...here. Just...in the spin cycle, I guess.

He kept smiling at the beer bottle, clinking the rings.

"We could make Narnia passports, dude."

I almost spat out, then swallowed, a mouthful of rum and coke.

"What's that?"

"Narnia passports. With a picture of Aslan on the front. We could design them and everything. I've got all the ideas in my head, I just need someone who's good at computers. We could make a million bucks, dude. People would go nuts over them. Think how great that'd be. The Foreign Minister's name could be Mr. Tumnus."

He smiled to himself and lit a cigarette.

"I really loved that book as a kid."

"I still do."

* * * * * * * * * * *

We sat for several hours and discovered we had many of the same favorite books and films until it was about noon.

"Would you mind doing me a small favor? I'll buy the beer all day if you just help me out for a few minutes."

"Sure. What is it?"

"I've got to go to the money wiring place to send some cash home to my daughter, or surrogate daughter, in Indonesia. I'm a couple of days behind and I can't stall out any longer, but I absolutely loathe going in there with all those forms with the tiny little spaces to write in. Look at my hands, dude."

They were shaking quite a bit.

"Yeah. You wanna go right now?"

"If you don't mind. After that we can come back and just drink."

"No problem."

We paid the bill, picked up a couple of beers at a shop and walked over to the Moneygram office.

When we got there, he half eased, half fell into a chair and got his reading glasses out of a pocket of his cargo shorts, opened his money belt, and began pilfering and muttering to himself. I smiled at the woman behind the glass, and asked for a form to send money abroad.

"Oh you're good, dude. Already on top of it. We gotta do this. After we get it over with, I'll be home free."

"Its no problem. We got all the time in the world..."

He tossed me his passport and held a piece of paper covered with scribbling close to his face. It was like he was looking at a cuneiform tablet.

"Here it is. My bank stuff. You'll need this."

He handed it over to me, knocking the beer sitting next to his feet over, quickly setting it back up and apologizing to the woman.

I began filling out the form with his information, starting with his name.

"Nice to meet you, Rupert."

"Oh yeah. What's your name?"

"Ian."

"Well how do you do, Ian? You got everything?"

"Yeah just give me a minute or two."

"It's ok dude. You're really doing me a favor here."

He punctuated half of his sentences with 'dude.' He would later tell me that 'The Big Lebowski' was one of his favorite movies and would constantly quote it, so I think that had something to do with it. Either way it sounded funny with his accent.

He leaned back, crossed his legs gingerly and sipped at his beer which was now all bubbled over. We got the first forms worked through to send the money. He didn't, in the least, seem perturbed at handing me all these details.

After about ten minutes we had it finished. The woman behind the glass was more than pleased to see that our business was finally wrapped up, and I handed him his passport and the paper with his bank details and addresses on it. He got up and bowed, thanking her. I did the same, and we were back out on the sidewalk. He seemed in very much better spirits.

"Alright! Where to? Back to the place?"

"Why don't we drink at the bar at my guesthouse? It's better."

We planted ourselves at the bar and Rupert ordered some beers.

"So you said that isn't your daughter that you sent money to?

"Well, no. Not technically. I've been like a surrogate father to her since she was about three. Her mother and I were together for several years, but she's all over the place. Sometimes she's around, sometimes she's not. Right now she is, because I'm not there, but she's not the most dependable person in the world. They stay at the grandmother's house though, who I can trust to take care of Mina."

"Is that her name?"

"Yeah."

"How old is she?"

"Nine. She'll be ten in a month, though. I can't wait for her birthday, dude. I've got the entire Chronicles of Narnia set to give to her. It's been driving me crazy to have it without giving it to her but I want it to be a meaningful present, so I'm waiting for her tenth birthday."

He ordered more beers for us and sat, smiling.

"It's pretty wild, dude. I'm not usually on the piss when I'm home. I use the times I'm away to get it out of my system. But I drank for years and years, everyday, through my twenties, thirties, forties. Then I met this woman and this little girl was a part of my life. You can't be drunk all the time around a little kid, dude. It doesn't work that way. I mean we all slip up, but...I don't want that for her."

He paused and lit a cigarette, then continued.

"When I was young, your age. I never thought anything in the world would keep me from getting absolutely rat-assed with my mates, every night. I used to make good money, working in the City of London, you know? It's like your Wall Street."

I nodded.

"Finance. We worked hard, and we played hard. A bottle of black label every night, dude. And, I had my ups and downs with it, with women, and all of that, and I never imagined I'd be sober for weeks, or ever months, at a time. For anything, or anyone. But, when I realized that I was responsible for that little girl, not because I'd put myself in a position to be, or was obliged to, but because I wanted to, it was actually pretty easy to stay clean. I never had anything beside myself that I cared about, other than making money, and that was just caring about myself. But when I realized that little girl needed me, and I knew I had to step up to the plate and be like a father, that desire to be out chasing women at bars and getting smashed... it just dissolved. It didn't matter to me.

"So, I fell in love with this woman, and I realized that what I wanted to do was to be there to help raise her daughter. Her grandmother does a lot, but they have no money. They have nothing. And I never wanted kids of my own. I never had kids with any woman, and I sailed right through that period of life where all my mates were making families, because it just never happened for me."

He took a drink from his beer.

"What I'm saying is that you've got to find something if you want to tame that dragon. It's not going to go away, and it's not going to leave you, but you can find a way to devote yourself to something other than yourself. It doesn't have to be some charity thing. Hell, I don't know how it'll be for you. But, that's how it was for me, dude."

He belched and we sat for a little while in silence, watching the headlines on the TV.

"Well, I don't really know about that, Rupert. I've got nothing to offer anyone in this state. Not even another adult, let alone a child."

"Yes you do. Yes you do, dude. You're a smart guy, and you've got a good heart. I can tell these things. You will have situations in your life that call you out of yourself, and your obsession with this" he held up the bottle. "And believe me, that's the way to overcome the beast. Changing your focus from yourself to something else. There are a million ways you can do something in the world to make someone else's life better, just one person. You can't change the world, or the big things. But, you'll be able to change someone's life for the better, and when you are given the opportunity, take it. I'm telling you now, it'll save your life. I wouldn't be here if it weren't for that little girl. It doesn't matter what suicidal, depressing shit I go through. When I sit and read her a bedtime story, I couldn't give a bollocks what happens to me. And that's how I stay sober. At least, when I'm home. When I get back I gotta climb the mountain and sweat all this out, dude. No more drinking for a while after these next two days."

I didn't have a clue what to say to that, and I didn't want to utter any cliches. I knew he was being straight up with me, and wasn't saying what he was saying because he wanted to be proud of himself. I could tell that he had been broken, and that he was finding a way to heal. He wasn't holding his head high and showing me what a great guy he was. I respected him for that, and the fact that he cared about my life enough to talk to me like that. I just didn't think I'd ever be anywhere near a situation to be there for anyone. I was in the process of becoming irretrievably unwound.

"Not much to do here, dude."

"It's a pretty sleepy little burg."

A few minutes went by, and he looked over at me slowly.

"You know what we need to do, dude?"

"What?"

"Let's go bowling."

"Really?"

"Yeah. There's a set of lanes just outside of town. It's amazing. They bring you this cart full of booze with buckets of ice and glasses, and you make them right there in the lane yourself. I can't believe I didn't think of it earlier!"

"I can't believe you didn't, either."

Chapter 15

Our tuk tuk sped through one and a half lane roads towards the sunset while Rupert talked about the bowling alley, as loudly as if we were on a speedboat.

"So, last time I went, there were only a few other people there, and we had free rein over the place. Wait'll you see it. It's my favorite place in Chiang Rai."

"I bowled a 67 the last time."

"That's pathetic, Ian."

We soon pulled up to the bowling alley and Rupert hurriedly shoved a handful of baht to the driver. If there were a black hole in my future, this was the most absurdly perfect reason to delay it by a day.

He scrambled up the front steps, turning around and screaming for me to hurry up, disappearing inside. When I got in, a cold rush of air-conditioning enveloped me.

"HERE WE GO! YOU SEE THIS? DO YOU SEE THIS?"

He put his arms out at his sides and turned around in circles like it was his newly-built mansion.

A small congregation of women whose unfortunate lot it was to deal with us for the next several hours came out from behind the shoe counter.

"Oh look at you, like a bird of paradise, you are. How lovely. We need a pair of shoes. And your best lane."

She motioned to the shoes like a game show hostess.

"Oh would you just look at all those shoes, Ian. What size are you?"

We got everything squared away and went down to the lane.

"Now: THE CART."

He hailed one of them over and gave instructions on what to bring. A few minutes later she wheeled over a metal cart with two liters of Sang Som, six bottles of coke, a large champagne holder full of ice, tongs, and several glasses.

"Mix us up a few, my boy," he said, holding a ball up in front of his face, slowly turning and studying it.

"Do you have your music with you?"

"Yeah. Why, you think they'd let us hook it up?"

"It'd be a lot better than this rubbish."

A Muzak version of "I Think We're Alone Now" was floating out from the speakers.

I got two drinks made for us, and took my iPod over to the woman working at the shoe counter. She let me come back and hook it up. I started up "London Calling," and when it came on I watched Rupert, sitting with his back to me waiting to begin, put both of his hands up in the air, as in supplication to the gods. I ran back down and he had his glass in the air.

"To life's rich pageant."

"To life's rich pageant, Rupert."

"If you can find a way to get up there, it's a sweet ride, baby! Airborne!"

Those words will remain with me forever.

We started throwing balls down the lane and neither showed any proficiency for the game. As seriously as Rupert took the whole experience, he really had no technique or any apparent amount of practice under his belt.

"Ah a six. Bollocks." He sat down and began making himself a drink.

"You know, Ian, it's really all just a game. I took it all so seriously for so long. I took what everyone around me thought and did, as well as what I thought and did, so seriously. We're always trying, aren't we? Sometimes we're trying to get as much money as we can, sometimes for love, sometimes for security, and sometimes for the respect of our family or our peers.

"I know you're going through some heavy existential shit, dude. I understand it. We drink just to be able to handle all of that. We've got the weltshmerz on our shoulders, don't we? And that can be a good thing, or a really obnoxious thing. I wouldn't try to give you some kind of advice because I'm older, because I couldn't stand any of that when I was a young man. But, I have learned a few things. Oh, good one Ian."

I threw one right in the gutter.

"Well, I don't doubt it, and I'd love to hear any insight you have."

He stood there in the lane, holding and sipping at the Sang Som and coke like it was the finest brandy in the world.

"I've seen people running around their whole lives trying to be happy. Some of them are, some of them aren't. Some of them have a lot of money, some of them don't. Some of them have large, loving families, and others are alone. But what I have noticed about happiness is that it comes to those who know how to... field it, I suppose is the word. Because you can't run after it, or from it. But you can't wait for it. It's hard to say but there's kind of a magical kind of state you can get in- no matter what you're doing- where you just kind of perfectly meet the universe halfway. That is airborne, son. That is airborne.

"There's also a kind of way that you can expect good things without expecting them, or want them without wanting them. Maybe it's better to think of it as being like making yourself a vessel for the good stuff, you know? You can't be hankering after happiness like a junky after smack, and you can't be living your life always concerned with whether it will come."

He took a drink.

"So, you can't be always worried about whether or not you deserve it or not, or whether you got a square deal or you got screwed...but you can't mope and deny to yourself that you need it. So, I just try to be aloof during the in-between, not-so-good times. But, when it does come, I try and spread it around as much as I can. That's the key. Being generous with it, giving it to people."

He threw his ball down the lane and got a strike. His arms went up in the air.

"Oh YEAH mama, it's a sweet ride! It is a sweet ride!"

For the next three hours we got absolutely tilted on the Sang Som, heaped exaggeratedly reverential accolades on the music we ran up to keep putting on, made each other convulse with laughter, and terrified the unfortunate other few who came for a night of family fun.

The last memory I have of that night is Rupert stumbling around in the back of the lane by the pins, playing air guitar on his knees and screaming "RUDI CAN'T FAIL....RUDI CAN'T FAIL.....RUDI CAN'T FAIL....."

* * * * * * * * * * *

The next morning I slogged out of bed, remembering bits of the insanity at the bowling alley from the night before. It made me aware of the fact that the strange was just around the corner, if you held yourself just right, and were open to it. It put me in a much more energized and positive head space. Rupert was an example of the kind of person I wanted to be when I was his age. I wanted that kind of absurdist zeal, that energy to just get up and go do things.

He had a jest in his manner that I deeply admired, and I realized just how wrapped up in my own nonsense I'd become. I wanted to always be the kind of person who jumped out of bed to see the sunrise every morning. I learned many lessons just from that first day with him. He was a stellar example that getting old doesn't mean getting jaded, bored, or burned out on life. I had absolutely no excuse to be so cynical.

It was time to figure out my next means of income as I was getting perilously down in the funds. When I would go to the ATM my hands would shake waiting for the sound it makes when its counting your cash, scared shitless every time that it would say 'insufficient funds.' I could be irrationally paranoid about that sort of thing. Though I was a fairly responsible drunk, I always woke up with the fear that the night before I had pulled out a hundred dollars and lost it in a tuk tuk or something.

I searched on the internet for English teaching jobs in Thailand, and it was much easier than I had thought to find one. I got in touch with a recruiting company who basically told me that as soon as I got down to Bangkok, they could find me a position somewhere in the country. I could deal with my existential crises later, as long as I knew I'd have an apartment in which to brood and drink. It was a major relief. I went over to see if Rupert was at Coconuts yet.

"Hey man, I didn't think I'd see you up so early."

"Couldn't sleep. Had to see what was going on with the Sumo scores."

"Sumo? Interesting..."

"I love it, dude. I was in Japan on business for a month in the eighties, and I was at a match every night. Instantly obsessed."

"Well I think I found some gainful employment. I need to get to Bangkok in a few days so I have enough time on my visa to get it extended, and it'll be a stretch money wise, but I think I can make it."

"I've got to be in Bangkok in three days for my flight back to Indonesia. Let's take the train."

"I was gonna take the bus, man. It's cheaper."

"Oh fuck the bus, dude. I'll get you a ticket."

"I couldn't do that, man."

"Yes you could. It's nothing. You've helped me out a lot in the past few days, writing emails and doing all that at the Moneygram office. I owe it to you. Plus, I know you're broke."

"Well, that's really cool of you, Rupert."

He motioned for a beer and I did as well.

"That means we should probably get down there soon."

"Yeah, I need to go tomorrow. Does that work for you?"

"It's perfect."

"Alright then, dude. We'll have one last day up here and then head out."

* * * * * * * * * *

Getting to Bangkok meant a three hour drive to Chiang Mai, then a night train. He had arranged a driver to get us down to Chiang Mai, and we left in the noontime. I watched the rolling hills and rice paddies jettison past as he slept nearly up until the minute that we rolled into the train station. We got there with precious few minutes to spare.

I had to grab another bottle of Sang Som at the 7-11 before we bought the tickets and found our platform, and that was really pushing it. At the counter, Rupert said he'd have first class and I asked the lady for a third.

"Nuh-uh, dude," he scoffed.

"Rupert, its fine, really. I am perfectly ok with a normal seat. I can't sleep on these things."

"If I'm buying the ticket, you're riding in first. There's no way I'm letting you ride in third or second. And that's that."

It was no use arguing with him. I acquiesced, got the cash out of his money belt which was hanging awkwardly around my neck, and paid the lady. He had me carry his important stuff because he was worried he'd lose it. We were off to the platform.

I was hurrying along to find our car and glanced back to see him taking his time, trudging along with his bag dragging along beside him, a boozy grin across his face. I showed my tickets to the guard at the door in time to hear his scream reverberate through the placid evening air at the station.

"WE'RE AIRBORNE, SON!"

He hoisted himself up onto the train which began moving, it seemed, as soon as he was completely aboard. The workers on the train were very excited to get us into our first class cabin. A chipper young man showed us to the room, shoved us in, and politely slid the door shut behind us. Rupert got right into bed and lied down.

I thought the chaos had mostly subsided. That the bed, the private cabin and the gently swaying train would cajole him to nod off to a fitful, thirteen hour sleep, to awake as we were just chugging into Bangkok station.

Making sure we had everything, I locked the door, climbed up into my cot, and laid there for about ten minutes. I was relieved to be on our way.

He was snoring away in his cot beneath me when the knock at the door started us both. The door slid open and a guy was there with menus to take our orders for dinner.

"Oh yeah, here we go," Rupert said, handing me one.

"Get whatever you want. Everything's good."

I doubted it. My gut instinct told me to go with the ham sandwich. There was little room for disease there.

"Two Changs, colder than a witch's cleft."

He accentuated that with a serious glance at the waiter.

"And I would love that red snapper plate. Ian, my man, you like red snapper?"

Even the sound of it almost made me vomit.

"I think I'll go with the ham sandwich."

The waiter scribbled it down and was off. Rupert lied back in his cot and kept talking about how great being in first class was.

"I know it, dude. You think when I was your age I'd ever get on first class? I was back with the proles in third. But now I appreciate it. This, this is the way guys like us need to go, dude."

"Hey don't get me wrong, it's fantastic. I've never been up here before. In fact, I've never been on a train in Asia. It was always buses."

"Whats the buses they have in the States? I had to ride that once."

"Greyhound. The dirty dog."

"GREYHOUND...god what a nightmare that is."

I hung over the side of the cot so I could see him.

"I once rode Greyhound for over sixty hours straight, from Kansas City to White River Junction, Vermont."

"Oh Jesus...I would have gone completely ape."

"It was pretty bad."

"I bet you saw some real freak shows on that ride!"

"It was like a demonic carnival."

There was a knock at the door and it slid open. Our food had arrived.

The guy handed me my plate, then set Rupert's red snapper down on the end of his cot. While I was hanging over the edge I could see his feet rise into the air a few inches as he tried to sit himself up, but then he slipped, and his feet fell back down, right into the middle of the fish.

He instinctively lifted them off of the plate and groaned, pieces of salad hanging off as he swung them onto the floor. The waiter's eyes went wide and he shoved the Changs at me, exiting the cabin.

Missing nothing, Rupert sat up and went to work on the snapper. I almost asked him to take his time because he was really barreling into it, but I just took a swig off the Chang, secured his between the wall and my mattress, and started eating. I thought of the strands of lettuce dangling precariously from his heel.

I handed him his Chang and he swigged it, handing it back to me. I put it back between the wall and mattress. In minutes he'd finished the fish, and set it on the ground by his feet. I handed him back his beer and he drained it.

"Not bad for a train! Better than what you'd get on a train back home, that's for sure."

"I'm loving this first class, man. I'm afraid I'll get spoiled on it."

"You will, dude." He belched. "Once you go black you never go back."

I laughed.

"Where's that rum? You brought it didn't you? Don't tell me we've got this whole bloody train ride with nothing but Thai piss!"

"Yep, right here." I fished in my bag and handed it down to him. He unscrewed the top and took a thirsty pull from it like it was Gatorade.

"I thought we'd at least get some mixers and ice, man! This is going to be fucking nuts, I know it. I hope we don't get kicked off."

"No...fun...no...fun...no...fun..." he musically reproached.

"Well, at least we've got our own cabin. It's a welcome change to be able to drink publicly without a carload of people staring the whole time."

"They can...fuck...right...off" he said and took another pull.

"Alright take it easy, that bottle has to be enough for both of us, remember!"

"Its all good, dude. We are . . . the . . . airborne."

I climbed down from my cot and went to take a leak and get some cans of coke and cups.

When I got back, the smell of vomit had permeated every pocket of air in the tiny cabin. Rupert was sitting on the edge of his cot, the bottle of rum sitting on the floor beside him.

"Jesus, are you alright?! Do the windows work?"

"Oh yeah. Let's get some air flow in here."

"What the fuck happened?"

"I lost that red snapper, dude."

"I can see that..." The sink, which wasn't hooked up to any water, was plastered across with puke. You could see the bits of fish. The smell filled my entire body and I thought I was going to lose it as well. I quickly grabbed a shirt out of my bag and tied it around my face to block some of the smell.

"You look like an al-Qaeda guy."

He chuckled to himself and sat back in his bed against the wall. I stepped over his legs to get to the window. I was standing right in front of the sink with the puke dripping down the front of it. I got the window open and the hot rush of air made the smell circulate more poignantly through the cabin.

"We've gotta do something about this, man. We're in here for upwards of eleven hours."

"Do you have some incense or something?"

"No...can we smoke in here?"

"They'll toss us off."

"Christ..."

The stench was going nowhere.

"Alright well I'm gonna get you some water and see if I can find something to wipe this up."

"Fuck it dude we'll be fine."

"I'm not looking at that all night, man. It's rancid."

"Why don't you just go change your diaper and chill out, dude."

"Alright, alright, alright. Are you ok?"

"I'm fine, dude. I just puked, I didn't have a heart attack."

He picked up the bottle of rum and took another drink.

"Ok, there's puke all up in *that* now."

"I didn't backwash."

He got up, taking a step towards the sink. He stood there momentarily, laughing to himself and swaying with the train, then put his hands on the sides of the sink and started to wretch again.

"Oh shit---"

His entire body tightened and braced, and he vomited again.

"OHHHH YEAHHHHHH" he growled, wretching several more times. "AIRBORNE, SON! WE ARE AIRFUCKINGBORN!"

He vomited again, waiting for the worst of the shaking to stop, and just stood there, still holding the edges of the sink.

"That snapper...oh god that snapper" he hiccupped and wiped his hands on his pants, turning around and picking up the rum off the floor. I reached for my beer and pulled the shirt tied around my face up to plug my mouth with the bottle, chugging the rest of it.

I watched in horror as he got back into position at the sink, one hand now to steady himself and the other holding the rum up, as in gratitude to Dionysus, as he swayed, took intermittent swills from it, wretched, and howled like a wolf.

"YOU BETTER BELIEVE IT! YOU HAD BETTER FUCKING BELIEVE IT!"

"Rupert, the rum's all getting wasted at this point! You're just gonna keep puking it up!"

"Yeah." He stood there in the middle of the cabin, looking at the bottle.

"We've still got plenty left for the ride, my boy. No way I'll handle going through the airport the least bit sober."

I hadn't even thought about that. I would surely have to be there for that.

"You'll be there, it'll be fine," he said, reading my mind. At last he gingerly placed the rum back on the floor and eased back onto his cot, sitting on the edge.

"I don't want to go back, dude. I've got too much shit to do back home. And I've gotta go to London sometime soon as well. Plenty to sort out there I've been putting off."

"It'll be fine."

"I know I know I know I know I know..." His voice faded as he leaned back and put his head on the pillow, his feet hanging off the edge.

"I want to thank you for everything, man, for getting me back to Bangkok and everything, and talking to me about my shit, and the bowling. You've really given me a different perspective on everything."

He sighed like someone had pulled a plank out of his chest.

"Just do something for someone else in the future who's in the same boat, that's all I ask."

"I won't forget...believe me..."

"Airborn, son. We're gonna get there. Fucking Bangkok."

I looked over the edge of my cot after a few minutes and saw that he was fast asleep. Trying to be as deft as possible in the tiny cabin, I crept out, almost forgetting to untie the shirt from my face. Staggering down to the food car, I bought several beers, and asked one of the workers for a blanket so I could cover up the puke that was still all over the sink and the wall.

When I arrived back at the room Rupert was on his side, in the fetal position, knocked out. We still had at least ten or so more hours to go, but I had basically gotten used to the smell, I realized to my disgust. I draped the blanket across the barf and scampered back up into the cot with my beers and found my book. It was going to be a long time before we got to Bangkok.

When we arrived at the train station, we had about two hours before Rupert's flight took off. Getting him there was a mission and a half. Luckily, he had slept almost all the way until the train groaned to a final stop, whereupon we gathered our things, I triple checked his money belt to make sure it had everything in it, and he plucked the Sang Som bottle out of the trash.

"Oh, Jesus fucking Christ. Really?"

"Dude, I won't do airports sober. Especially Bangkok. That place is a nightmare."

"Well, just make sure you can get on the plane, for Chrissake!"

"Why do you think I'm going to the fucking airport, for fuck's sake?"

We got a taxi to Suvarnaphumi and talked old movies and other subjects we had shared over the past two weeks. I took him with his things up to the Air Asia desk and he got his boarding pass, and while we were walking around trying to find where he should go through security, he was making jokes about being a terrorist, at a volume that was well within earshot of people we walked past.

"I'm Al-Qeada, dude. I'm gonna put a bomb in your ass, dude. I'm Osama bin Laden!"

He would cackle while I begged him to shut up. I was genuinely scared at that point that he'd be arrested. All of a sudden he stopped and began fishing around in his money bag. He pulled out several thousand baht and handed them to me.

"Rupert, you don't have to do that, man. That's really-"

"Take it." He shook the bills in mid-air.

"Man, that's incredibly generous of you but-"

"You've got what, several days here before you'll start a job? What are you gonna do, eat ramen and drink out of the tap? No way. Take it."

"Rupert, I really appreciate that but-"

He lowered his head so we were eyeball to eyeball. "Shut up, dude."

I took the bills from him. He smiled.

"I can wire this to you as soon as I get a paycheck, I promise, man."

"Bollocks! If you must, send it to Children of Sumatra. Give a kid a cleft-palate operation. Change their life forever. We got it good, dude. Don't forget that. We got it nice and good."

I knew that if heaven existed, his mansion there was getting new wings by the day.

"Thank you, Rupert."

"Do amazing things, Ian. Don't forget, you are airborne."

"Take care, buddy. I'll be speaking with you real soon."

He waved and lumbered off through security. I could see him horsing around with the metal detector people and I prayed to all the gods that existed that he made it through the flight and back home, without getting arrested.

Chapter 16

My wait for a job in Thailand yielded to my will quicker than I expected. I had been watching a ceiling fan turn at a guesthouse off of Koh San Road for only three days before I was in a car to Nakhon Ratchasima province. The job was in Korat, the third biggest city in the country, but not a place that many tourists go.

Although this may be a selling point for some, Korat is one of the places where it isn't. Tourists don't go there because there is not much reason to. One advantage of this is that it is probably a much better example of the 'real Thailand' than other places more visited by tour buses. The businesses and general infrastructure of the city are not built around or supported by tourist money, and the visitor will most likely feel that it is a more genuine experience of how normal people live in that country.

The job I signed a contract for was at a high school. We went to meet the director and my only other Western co-worker, a middle-aged American guy who was full of stories about his time in the army, how liberals were ruining the whole world, and how Barack Obama was a socialist Muslim.

The owner of the recruiting agency drove me to a couple of apartment houses so I could find a room, and I took one that was $50 a month. It had a bed and a dresser, a fan on the ceiling, and in the bathroom, a shower spigot and a toilet. No sink. I immediately got stale and depressing vibes from it but the woman who rented it seemed sweet and it was only a few minutes' walk from the school, which would save me on transportation. After exchanging some information with the recruiter, he drove back to Bangkok and I went upstairs to my new room.

A depressing pall was cast across everything. I was glad to have a paycheck again, and a place to live, and all that, but it was a very difficult first night. I had never felt that averse to a new place, and on top of it I felt incredibly lonely. Some places just feel lonelier than others, no matter if there are people around or not.

I had never experienced loneliness because I was alone. I was more likely to feel lonely when I was with someone I didn't connect with than when no one was around. But this was another beast. It was psychically oppressive. I walked down to the shop on the first floor of the building, got the day's edition of the Bangkok Post, a bottle of Sang Som, a can of coke and a plastic cup, and went upstairs to start saturating myself.

I awoke in the middle of my first night there to rain coming in through the ceiling, all over the bed. I must have been absolutely annihilated because the mattress was already completely soaked through. I was slipping around on the floor and cursing, trying to move the bed out from under the corner of ceiling that, I now noticed, was brown and rotted through with an apparent history of leakage.

I laid back down on the wet mattress, livid, waiting for the sun to rise.

I finally got up at seven, took a cold shower with several big-toe-sized cockroaches, brushed my teeth over the bucket, and put on my one outfit which was work appropriate. There was no excitement about starting the new job or being in a new city, which was atypical of me.

The classes went alright. In fact, during the several months that I would be there, the time I spent teaching would be the only that I would find real enjoyment. My students were in the last two grades of high school and I got to teach basically whatever I wanted. It also gave me much insight into the general state of Thai culture, as teaching kids in any country allows. They showed a healthy curiosity with the rest of the world and a desire to strike out and know about other cultures, which I found inspiring.

My co-worker, a mustachioed, middle-aged, former military man from Klamath Falls, OR, was a complete freakshow. On my first day, he told me stories of two different times that he had murdered someone. Once when he was in Vietnam, and another time when he was working as a security guard, transporting prisoners to and from California state penitentiaries. He would stand behind me while I read my email, looking at it over my shoulder, and refer to any news site I went to as "socialist crap."

Not that he was a bad guy. Underneath his Bill O'Reilly and John Birch-derived socio-political outlook, his constant supply of pointless advice, army anecdotes, and his creepy interactions with students, he was actually a good person. He lent me a thousand baht once a couple of days before my first payday, invited me over for dinner a couple of times, and was in a cheery and uplifting mood most of the time, when he wasn't talking about murdering his girlfriend.

It's just that every time he opened his mouth my patience was taxed to its limit. I felt like I was in some kind of yogic training camp which threw a million reasons to be annoyed in my face every day, and I had to develop more ingenious ways of surmounting them and controlling my mind. And in that regard, spending all of those afternoons with him may have been very much a blessing. It also gave me plenty to laugh about after I had gotten off of work, and at the time gut laughs were like precious metals.

There really was nothing to do there. The few expat bars were frequented by lurid older guys, and you had to wonder why they ended up in a place like Korat. It was obvious many of them weren't working there, and maybe they had wives from the area, but the mood was downright creepy.

Most of them seemed miserable, and expressed all of the latent racism and bitterness so common to scenes like that. It wasn't strange to see them yelling at their wives in front of the whole bar or storming around acting like children. For these reasons, and because I had little cash and no one to go see, I spent nearly all my nights in Korat at the apartment.

At first I spent every night reading the paper as well as the biggest books I could find, like a university textbook about the history of Europe I had found. I would also pace a lot. I felt more like Travis Bickle every day. Eventually I was able to put together enough cash for a secondhand Samsung tablet which allowed me to use the internet and listen to podcasts.

The weekends were the worst. I would walk all over the city, trying to find some hole in the wall bar, or venue, or any place that didn't feel like a den of reprobates to spend time in away from my tiny, moldy apartment. It was to no avail.

I once went out to get drinks with this American woman who worked in another department at my school. Things went alright for the first hour or two, but I had drunk too much before I met up with her. Later in the evening, at an expat bar, I had evidently stood up on a stool and told everyone they were "the most depressing assholes" I'd ever seen in one place. After I left, I got into the backseat of a Thai woman's car as if it were a taxi, and the American woman had to pry me out and put me in a tuk tuk. She had to tell me all this, of which I was blissfully unaware, at lunch the following Monday. Things were becoming unmanageable.

And I was absolutely miserable. Never before in my life had I been in such despairing, dark straits. I had many months left to my contract, and although many days I tried to tell myself that I would stick it through, that I should just grow some balls and make it happen until I could get a new job somewhere I wanted to be, I was losing my will by the week. It was like being pushed and held down in a swamp. If there were people there I could spend quality time with, have fun with, converse with, it wouldn't have bothered me that my surroundings were so arrestingly devoid of beauty. I knew I wouldn't meet anyone I connected with there, and that every night I would be at my shitty apartment, pacing back and forth, drinking a liter of Hong Thong a night.

After weeks of this I became irretrievably depressed and lost it one night, at about four o clock in the morning.

I decided to just get the hell out of there. I got to a crisis point I'd never been at before. I didn't even really stop to think about anything. The only thing I could think of was going back down to Koh Tao, where this whole thing started. I completely lost any semblance of self-control, and I didn't really see any other option. The plan I quickly arrived at was to go down, get a bungalow, buy a whole load of Diazepam and enough rum to kill a platoon, have the best time I could with the last of the money I had, and have a fatal accident.

Chapter 17

As the pre-dawn sky was turning a silvery-blue, I got the things I needed packed into my bag, left the key in the door, picked up a bottle of Sang Som downstairs, and walked into the street. After stopping by the ATM and taking everything I had out, leaving one baht in the account, I got a tuk tuk to the bus station and bought a ticket leaving in ten minutes. I grabbed a plastic bottle of coke, poured out a third of it in the street, filled it back up with rum, and perched myself at the back of the bus. Given the circumstances, I was in incredibly light spirits. It felt like a massive weight had been lifted off of me to be leaving that city, that apartment, that job, and all the hopeless miasma I had waded in for the past three months.

I don't remember very much of the ride to Bangkok. I was just destroyed on booze and I am surprised that I was able to navigate myself all the way to the Sawasdee House, a place I had stayed at several times before. I wasn't even planning on spending the night there, because I knew that night buses would be leaving for Surat Thani that evening, and it was only about 10am when I got to Bangkok. I breezed into that lobby that I loved so much, where I had stayed when I came to Thailand for the first time nearly a year before.

When I went to the travel desk at the guesthouse, the woman said the rides to Koh Tao were all full. I thought that was unlikely, and kept pushing her to try more companies or other outlets, but she was adamant that there were no more buses going south that evening and that I would have to try again tomorrow. In my state I just took her word for it, and didn't walk around and try to buy a ticket at one of the other million ticket shops in the vicinity. I would later find out that she hadn't sold me a ticket because I was so inebriated.

I walked around Koh San for a little while, and eventually went back to the Sawasdee House, checked into one of their closet sized, windowless single rooms, and passed out.

When I woke up I had no way of knowing what time it was. I decided I would go down and check out the scene in the lobby. It had only been a few hours, evidently, because when I got down there, it was night time.

That lobby was one of my favorite rooms in the city. There were all the predictable acoutrements of design you would expect of a backpacker hostel in Bangkok- reclining buddhas, lamps made from the sea's flotsam and jetsom, furniture from driftwood, framed landscapes on the walls that looked like 1940s postcards, curios, various implements from ships and other bits of exotica.

It was a beautiful expanse of room, lit by red, green and yellow lights, which opened completely onto Rambuttri where people were smoking shisha, drinking Changs and fending off the more tenacious trinket sellers. A pool table was up on an elevated area next to the kitchen, a giant wooden mermaid hanging overhead. The wait staff were running around all over the place and I flagged one down for a rum and coke as I sat up near the pool table, studying the room's habits.

After several minutes, I noticed a woman sitting across the lobby at the travel desk from which I had tried to buy my bus ticket earlier.

I don't know what it was, but she became the only person in the room.

I had never seen her before, yet I was certain that I had known her my entire life.

I knew it wasn't because I thought she was pretty, because I wasn't even close enough to her to see clearly when I had this feeling. Maybe it was the way that she gesticulated to the travel agent, or the earnest way she was sitting, or her facial expressions. I don't know, but I'd never been affected just by seeing a woman like that, and I'd looked at a million gorgeous women before. This was something else. I was drawn right over to her.

I rose, picked up my drink, and walked across the lobby to the travel desk. I sat down next to her, like a moth to a flame.

I could hear that she was going to Hanoi so I began talking to her about it, and all of the things I loved about it. She was a little taken aback at first, but seemed very friendly. I was really excited to interact with her. It felt as though she was a close friend, who I hadn't seen for a very long time. It was remarkably easy to speak with her. Soon she finished up with the travel agent.

She was tall and slender, with elbow-length brown hair and a face with delicate yet angular features, like a serious person who smiles often and easily. Her eyes were green and piercing, and seemed otherworldly yet so close to home.

The travel desk was inside the lobby, and adjacent to it was a seating area, under the enigmatic gaze of the wooden mermaid.

"Would you like to have a drink?"

She smiled and said "sure," and picked up her bag.

Her face, the energy she gave off, her auric field, seemed so familiar. Like stepping into a recurring dream...

"Really? Ok, that's nice. Let's head over there, shall we?" I kind of pointed with my drink.

After we got seated, she asked what I was drinking.

"A rum and coke."

"Yeah, that sounds good."

I called over the waiter and ordered us a couple. She was watching me with a kind of apprehensive amusement, like one would watch a wild animal dancing around in a dress at the circus. I think she didn't quite know what to think. She leaned forward and put her elbows on the table.

"What's your name?"

"Ian. What's yours?"

"Elena."

I was thinking the whole time how oddly nice it felt to be sitting there with her. It wasn't just because I thought she was beautiful, or that I liked the sound of her British accent, or something like that. It was definitely something else.

She asked me what I was doing there. My only fear was that she would think I was looking for sympathy, but at that point I had nothing to lose.

"I'm headed down to Koh Tao, to drink myself into a hole in the ground."

She nodded and raised her eyebrows, looking into my eyes the whole time.

"Why?"

"Because the world's a disgusting place, and I'm just tired of being a part of it. I know its weak, I know it's cliche, but it's the truth. There's no way I'll be able to dig myself out of the hole I'm in. I don't have a future. I never thought I'd make it to thirty, anyways. It's not posturing, but a definite intuition.

I'm cooked. I'm ready for the next trip. Put me on the spaceship and send me home."

"What about your family?"

"I'll feel terrible for them, but they don't have anything to do with this."

"Your friends?"

"Again, I will miss them dearly, but this is beyond all of those kinds of concerns."

She sat back, holding my gaze. She was remarkably casual, but direct.

"Well, fair enough. I can understand, I guess."

She took a drink.

"But, I really doubt you've thought it all through."

"Yeah, well...hmm. Maybe."

The existential inferno that had been clawing through my veins since I left Korat was, and this was very strange, comforted. *Well, here's something quite nice.*

I waved my hand and shook my head, to get us off the subject of why I was in Bangkok. We talked about Thailand and our experiences there, and the things we loved about it and all of its funny peccadilloes. It was refreshingly easy to make her laugh.

She was extremely pleasant to look at, but in a way that was very quizzical to me, like 'oh, so this is what you look like! How fascinating...' Looking at her face, her high cheekbones and directed gaze, a stranger had never seemed so familiar. I felt like my dearest friend in the world was sitting right across from me, and I was just about to get to know her!

I finally felt like I could relax. It was like I'd been lugging around some huge suitcase and finally was able to set it down and take a breather. Or, like I'd been riding around on a dark subway for years, and a voice finally screamed out 'ok- this is your stop!'

In some parts of northern California and Arizona, there are vortices, where ley lines and other energetic fields intersect and create powerful spots on the surface of the Earth. I've never gone to a vortex, but the way it felt sitting at a little table with her in that bustling guesthouse lobby is the best understanding I have of them.

"So, how long are you here for?"

"Two days."

"Well, that's the same as me! Of course, I have a more open schedule than you. Are you here with anybody? Are you, you know...with a guy?"

"No. Are you here with anyone?"

"Not for a while."

I flagged one of the waiters down and ordered another round for us.

I didn't want it to seem as if I was even trying to be smooth or anything, not that that was difficult in my stained Carhartts and Crocs, but I really wasn't trying to impress her in any way. There really wasn't a reason to, at that point. I just liked being around her. Everyone else in the world seemed like a stranger. I knew that a woman like her probably got hit on a lot, and I would lob off a finger before she thought I was just trying to get into her pants. Because I wasn't. I just didn't want to scare her off. Either way, she didn't seem to assume I was merely hitting on her.

I wanted to spend the day with her. I didn't think it was too much to ask. I thought that if the universe would just give me the day with her, she would see what a nice friend she'd just met. I just knew.

Eventually I asked her if she'd like to check out this restaurant with me the next night.

"It's very cool. I went there the last time I was here. The food is quality, not like your typical tourist place with the laminated, five hundred item menu. It's like health food, all vegetarian."

"Sure." She smiled.

"Really? Ok...well, when's a good time? I'm thinking like...five."

"Ok."

You gotta go for it.

"Well if you're not doing anything earlier, we could walk around the area, you know, make a day of it."

"Yeah, alright." She was nodding slowly and studying me, smiling.

"Yeah? Great! Perfect. Ok so probably like...eleven?"

"How about one. I'm knackered..."

"All right! One it is! Yes. Would you like another drink?"

"No, I don't think I do. I need to get some sleep after the past few days. See you tomorrow, though?"

"Oh yeah. One o'clock. I'll totally brush my teeth."

* * * * * * * * * *

The next morning, I awoke with no way of knowing what time it was, panicking that I had tragically overslept. I struggled in my freshly awake state to get my jeans and shirt on, and jogged to the stairs.

I heaved a sigh of relief as I saw that she was sitting in the lobby, and walked right up to her table. She looked up and smiled, slightly startled.

"Good morning! How are you?"

"Fantastic. Never better. And yourself?"

"Yeah. Good. I've been in Hong Kong for a week and I never get any sleep when I'm there. So, I'm slowly catching back up."

"Is that where you live?"

"No, I just go every few months for work. But I used to live there."

"So didn't you say last night that you're from the Congo?"

"Well, I was born in South Africa, but my mum's British and I went to school in England."

"You grew up in England?"

"No I grew up in Zaire, or now the Democratic Republic of the Congo."

"That's interesting."

"Yeah, my mum had moved to South Africa from England, and married my dad, who was South African. He died when I was two, so-"

"Jesus, I'm sorry to hear that."

"Oh, I was so young. Some years later, she married a guy who was in the diplomatic service in Zaire so I mostly grew up there. I moved to England for school when I was nine, and we also lived in Paris for a couple of years. And then I moved to Dublin, for college."

"There are a million questions I have about all of that."

A server came by and set an omelet on the table.

"Do you want anything?"

I ordered a coffee.

We chatted on like that while enjoying the morning's refreshments and the breezy lobby. She was the most uniquely ravishing woman I had ever the pleasure of sitting across from.

"Well, would you like to go take a stroll?"

"Sure!"

All of the usual street hawkers were in full effect that mid-morning, such as the guys selling suits and oversized novelty lighters, hill tribe women selling wooden frogs that make a croaking sound, sleeves that make your entire arm look tattooed, and the northern Indian fortune telling men.

I had walked down this loop many times in the past year and it always seemed like the fortune telling men remembered me. One of them always came up to me when I was walking by and said "hello lucky man. You are a lucky man. You have lucky face." Then later he would say "You are the lucky face man. Funny face, also. Very lucky and funny face." Then I would do another loop and come back around and he would say, more sternly "do you like it when I call you the lucky man? The lucky, funny face man? Do you like it when I call you funny face? When I say that you are the lucky and funny face man? *Do you like that?*"

There is a nice scenic loop you can take down Rambuttri to Koh San, then almost all the way down until you get to an alley way with a sign that says "Boston Tailor." If you keep going through that alley you will end up clear at the top of Rambuttri again, and you can head all the way down and back to Koh San Rd.

It was fascinating for me to watch her walk around that circus while we talked enthusiastically back and forth. There was a freshness, a playfulness in her manner, almost childlike, yet she was slightly shy, contained, and elegant in her own odd way. It was as though the events and phases that inevitably make people jaded and cynical had just passed over her, never touching her. I was riveted by this creature.

We were gawking at stuff but neither of us were into buying anything. I definitely had as much stuff as I needed, and she had obviously sailed through these mountains of trinkets and tee shirts a million times before. It was nice to walk around though. There was a tiny bar right there in the alley I mentioned that is one of my favorites in the world. I suggested we take a pit stop there for a tropical beverage.

"So what's going on with Australia? You mentioned something about it last night."

"Oh, I've been dealing with an outrageous, ongoing debacle with immigration there. I first moved there over a year ago because I had wanted to move there since I was little. For some reason, I always wanted to live in Sydney. It always seemed right. Also, I thought that it would be a fresh, exciting scene design-wise. Anyways, I found a visa consultant, and began going about opening up a shop in the city."

The old woman dropped off our My Thais, never taking her eyes off of the soap opera on the TV above the table.

"Well, this consultant turned out to be an absolute moron. In fact, anyone who had anything to do with immigration did as well. Months went by and hardly anything was done about my case. When I would contact them, they acted as if they were busting their asses all day, but nothing would ever actually happen. It would take weeks for them to read a single document. It was like something out of the movie Brazil. They were too dense to understand, for instance, a training plan I submitted and some other things about the business, but the consultants kept going with it the entire way, so I never thought there was a problem. But there was never any progress. I would think there would be, and then they would just ask for another document, over, and over, and over.

"Sounds like a nightmare."

"I know. After I realized I was getting hosed by these consultants, I hired a lawyer who specialized in immigration. He took on the case and I thought things would improve. They haven't yet. I mean, how difficult can this be?"

"So what will you do now?"

"Well, I've been in this situation for well over a year now, and the past several months have been ridiculous. My shop is still there, and I am paying a stupid amount for rent and utilities, as well as having to pay salaries for two part time workers but I can't get back in to actually run it. I finally had to leave about a week ago and have since been in Hong Kong, working on some apartments, but this Sydney situation is completely draining. I couldn't even get back in to close my shop if I needed or wanted to at this point. Not even as a tourist."

"And what does the lawyer say about the future of your case?"

"Well he acts like it is going to go through any day, but it's been three months since I hired him and nothing's happened. We're always at a milestone moment in the deliberations, but then they need another document, or they need to have another meeting. So, I don't know when I will be able to go back. That's why I am on my way to Hanoi, to see if I can find materials for some new pieces I want to make. Hopefully it'll go through soon."

"God, that's rough. It must be awful with these bureaucratic imbeciles fumbling around with your future."

"Tell me about it. I don't know when I'll be able to live somewhere. I'm basically just wandering around Asia, trying to be productive in the meantime. I need to land somewhere though. I won't have anywhere to live until they make up their minds. I've been optimistic about it so far, but I don't know how long I can put up with it..."

We finished the drinks and decided to drop some stuff back at the Sawasdee House, and then go out for the evening.

* * * * * * * * * * *

We got to Ethos and took our shoes off, sitting down on some cushions on the floor.

"So, there's really not a man in your life?"

"The last boyfriend I had was for four years. He was a great guy, but eventually I had to end it."

"When was that?"

"Mmmm...let me think...three years ago? Wow...time goes by..." she said, her eyebrows furrowed.

"We moved to Hong Kong, and I was able to set up a fairly successful business designing furniture there. I became pretty unhappy, though. It was just too commercial for me. The entire mindset of the place is built around money. Finance, portfolios, stocks. At first there were many things that interested me about Hong Kong. It's very vibrant, cosmopolitan, with tons of opportunities, but it eventually turned into a nightmare. I had a thing with a few guys there, but it never lasted more than a couple of months. They have women throwing themselves at them because they're all cashed up, but all they seem to care about is their portfolios. They've lost the plot. And frankly when I was living there, I did too. And I was increasingly aware of the...soullessness of the place. None of the values that are really important to me seemed to exist in that environment.

"It's impossible to keep your feet on the ground. I mean, practically speaking, also. You are so far from the Earth, as the city is so tiny geographically, but so densely packed with skyscrapers of people all living on top of one another. The cost of real estate goes up with each floor. But when you look out at the other windows you just see how futile it all is. By the time you have got to the top there will always be another newer, taller building, and the city is just full of people scrambling to get to the top."

The server came over and we ordered the veggie burger and the Mediterranean plate, to share.

"Like, I said, these guys I was seeing were making loads of cash. I would never have had to worry about money or any of that. If I'd stayed with one of them, things would have been very secure, stable, our futures more or less planned out. I was also able to do what I loved, which is one of the most important things for me. But there was something missing from the situation, something that became larger and looming with every passing month. I didn't want to spend the rest of my life in a place where it seemed being rich was the most important thing. It became deadening. There was no spark. Eventually I moved to Australia to start a business and open a shop there."

"Well, I'm just glad to hear that you left when you decided that it wasn't right for you. It's...inspiring to hear that. Many people in your situation, with all that security and whatnot, would have stayed in it and tried to repress or ignore the psychological and spiritual things that were troublesome. But therein lies death, spiritual death, I think."

"Yeah, I agree."

"It takes some balls to walk away from all of that and transplant yourself to somewhere completely new."

She nodded. "Yeah. It does..."

After dinner we went to some bar that had a ridiculous band playing and had a load of drinks. We eventually left because we felt bad about laughing the whole time while they were playing 80's ballads.

We wandered around all over Rambuttri and got drinks at a bunch of different places before eventually winding up back in the lobby of the Sawasdee House.

After some playfully awkward banter we went up to my room.

My guardian angel probably masturbated for the next hour.

Chapter 18

I was wrested from sleep several hours later, enraptured. Elena's head and arm were across my chest. I couldn't believe how well we'd got on the day before. It was just like we'd been together for years, had to separate, and then were reunited. It was utterly uncanny.

She began to stir on the tiny bed and smiled.

"Aw, Ian..." She wrapped her arms around me.

"How are you?"

"I'm incredible. You?"

"Marvelous." We squeezed each other.

"What time is it?"

"About noon."

"What time do you think we went to sleep?"

"Probably around seven, I would imagine. We didn't get up here until like two."

She yawned, causing me to yawn.

"Elena, I had one of the most fantastic days of my life yesterday..."

"Ohh....me too, Ian, me too..."

"How about we go get some breakfast?"

"Absolutely. Where do you want to eat?" I was kissing her stomach.

"Oh, just downstairs is fine. I'm not fussed."

We slowly got dressed, exhausted and languid. She was radiant and I was basking in the glow of finding such fortune, finding such a friend. Everything she did was a treat to watch. Every mannerism came from a genuine and confident place. A confidence that was unconcerned with itself, with nothing to prove, no one to outdo. There was nothing phony about her. We might have been ten years old. All the fetters and scabs of experiences past fell away, and something gorgeous was peering through from underneath.

At breakfast we ordered that stalwart of backpacker nosh, greasy omelets and fruit smoothies. She made a proposition.

"You know, there's this one beach on Koh Phangan, and no one is ever there. It's my favorite place in Thailand, one of my favorite places in the world. There's only like two or three sets of bungalows on it, no roads, no motorbikes, hardly electricity. And, it's the most beautiful beach I have ever seen. I think we should go! Just for a few days. I think we could both really use it. It could be really, really nice!"

"That's the kind of thing I don't need to think about for longer than a nanosecond."

"Ok, well I think we should go today!"

"What about your Vietnam ticket? Don't you leave tomorrow?"

"I've already thought about that. I can get it pushed forward several days. I've definitely gotta be back here in two weeks to fly to the UK for a friend's wedding, but I don't really have to be in Hanoi for anything in particular. I'll still have plenty of time there after the beach, and I think this is just...a really good idea." It was so exciting just to sit across from her. I felt like this was all of my birthdays rolled into one.

After breakfast we went to the travel desk and tried to get a ticket on that night's bus. They were all booked up, so we got them for the next night. Then there was the question of our rooms. It was already 11:30, and we were both in windowless singles. That wasn't going to work. I went to reception and enquired. They had a double with a private shower and AC.

"We'll take it."

We got the key for the new room and moved our stuff into it. As far as I was concerned, it might've been a palace.

I grabbed a bottle of Sang Som and a pack of cigarettes from the lobby and returned to the room. I made us drinks and we both took showers while excitedly sharing our life stories, like we were getting caught up after many years apart.

She sat on the bed and I began going through my bag.

"I've never seen anyone traveling with such a little bag."

"Yeah and you know what? I don't even need some of this stuff. I hate having stuff I don't need. Like this shirt. Its long sleeved, with a hood. My friend gave it to me but I'll never need it out here. I don't know why I ever took it with me, except that I really like it." I thought for a minute and threw it in the laundry bin.

"One of the cleaning ladies can have it."

"Don't you think you'll want it when you go back home?"

"I have no designs on going back home."

"Fair enough."

We hung out in the room for several hours. I went down to the bar periodically to get glasses of ice and cans of coke for the rum.

"You drink a lot."

"Yeah. I told you that."

"Do you always drink this much?"

"Yeah. Usually. So tell me about your business and what you do."

"A major part of it at the moment is designing and manufacturing furniture out of reclaimed, eco-friendly materials. So, I go to places like Chatuchat market here, as well as Chiang Mai and all over Bali, to find beautiful pieces of old boat wood, pieces from temples and houses that have been torn down, driftwood, railway sleepers, and so on, and make furniture out of them. I've been doing that for several years now. One of the things that I'm keen to do now, which I've been working on developing in the past six months or so with different engineers in Australia, is a hemp furniture line. There are a couple of guys I've been working with, one of them is a complete mad scientist, but the main issue is finding the best ratio of magnesium oxide to hemp in order to maximize the structural integrity of the furniture."

"Wow. That's gnarly."

"I love working with it. It's the miracle plant. It yields four times what paper trees do per acre. It requires comparatively less water, zero pesticides, and is really good for the soil surrounding it. It's one of the strongest natural fibers on the Earth, and the entire plant can be used for so many things. You can make a house out of a compound made from hemp that is very similar to concrete. It's completely carbon negative, just as strong, and when it gets bulldozed, there is only organic material left in the rubble."

"That's incredible. An entire house made out of the stuff."

"Yeah, so...we've been working to find a way to get furniture made out of it, and if I could just spend a few months working with those engineers, I'm positive we could begin manufacturing pretty groundbreaking stuff. But, thanks to the Kafkaesque doings of the Australian immigration office, I can't be there to monitor the process and keep the whole thing running."

"That's really amazing though. It's so refreshing to meet someone with such enthusiasm in what they are doing and what they want to do. I would love to see some of your stuff."

"Well I'd love for you to see it as well. Hopefully soon I can go back to Australia and work at my shop again."

We horsed around in the room for a little while and had a few more drinks. For dinner we went out to an Indian restaurant around the corner, wolfing down a delightful sundry of dishes so spicy my scalp screamed. Absolutely wrecked from being up most of the night, we went back to the room.

After some excited yet sleepy interrogation about this beach we were off to the following day, we fell asleep easily.

Chapter 19

The next morning at breakfast I suggested we get a guitar.

"We have to have a guitar if we're gonna be loafing around a desert island bungalow for several days. I got the entire beach bungalow catalogue in my head, baby."

"Well let's get a guitar then!"

Walking around the area, I picked up a beautiful acoustic guitar. We couldn't think of anything else we needed.

"There's a few gift things I could get but there'll be plenty of opportunity in Vietnam, I'm sure."

Neither of us wanted to think about her leaving.

We went back to the Sawasdee House and put her bag in storage, except for a few things she put in my bag.

"Really? That's all?"

"Yeah. I don't need anything. Just a couple of dresses and a toothbrush, and my bikini."

"The thought is causing blood to rush to my penis."

She laughed, looking about at the tables of people around us.

"I'm serious. It's rushing right in there."

The van came to pick us up to take us to the station, and we got settled in our seats for the night journey. I prayed fervently that we could have as many days together as the universe would be so gracious to allow.

* * * * * * * * * *

It was another shock to see how spontaneous, adventurous, and adaptable she was. I had never known a person with whom it was such a pleasure to travel. She didn't complain or seem to be bothered by anything. All of the little things that people fuss about, when on night buses, or darting around trying to find the right van or tuk tuk to this or that place, didn't occur to her. She gracefully swam through everything.

We got to Surat Thani, and then the catamaran to Koh Phangan. She laid in my lap as I sipped on a Chang while she told me all about this place she was taking me to, where she had been several times before.

"I really wanted to go back here, from the second I got to Bangkok a couple of days ago, but never, ever thought I would be. I've never met someone while I was traveling that I could do this with."

The boat whipped and bounced along as we held each other on the hard plastic bench.

When we got to Koh Phangan we eschewed the Full Moon Party outpost of Haad Rin Bay for the north end of the island, which we reached by truck. When we got up there a woman sitting nearby came running up and asked us if we needed a boat. She yelled at a guy sleeping in a fishing boat. He jumped up, put on his hat, helped us into the boat, and fired up the motor.

A half hour later we bobbed into a very magnificent place, a parentheses-shaped strip of beach about a kilometer long, framed on either side by jagged rock.. Palm trees covered the hills which began rising almost immediately from the white sand. I looked at Elena, wide-eyed. She flashed a smile at me like we had made it home after a long journey.

We got the bag and the guitar out of the boat, hopping onto the sand.

"Oh Ian I'm so excited to be back here!" She was bouncing up and down and clutching my arm as we walked up the beach. Approaching a restaurant on stilts with flags fluttering in the wind, she said "Ok, this is the place. I'll get it sorted."

"Fantastic."

She stepped inside and negotiated for a few minutes, returning with a key, grinning.

"Let's go!"

We climbed up the tree-shaded hills off of the beach and found our place. It was a small, simple thatch hut with a front porch and a postcard view of the ocean. I set our bags down and followed her into the room. We stood and wrapped ourselves around one another.

"This sort of thing doesn't happen to me..."

"But it *is* happening to you. Wanna go for a little dip?"

We got changed and traipsed down to the beach, Elena barefoot over the brambles, rocks, and prickly things from the trees. When we waded into the crystalline water, she started talking about how we could exfoliate in the sea.

"This is the best way to do it. The sand and saltwater are so good for your skin. Here. Take some sand and just rub it all over."

We sat in the water and started rubbing it over our shoulders, arms, stomachs.

"Don't hold back. Scrape all those years of intoxicants off."

"I read in an old yogic book that we should think of our skin like a second pair of lungs, and imagine breathing through our pores just as we do our lungs. It said the best way to bathe was to use a boar's hair brush and lukewarm water, to open your pores up every day."

"Well when we met you definitely didn't look like you'd gone to the trouble of a boar's hair brush. Or even water."

"If you'd seen my bathroom in Korat you wouldn't have gone in there either."

We swam out into the water. It was clear enough to see our feet below, as if we were standing on the ground. I had never seen water that clear. After being sufficiently salty we got out and sat on some cushions at the restaurant.

"I'm starved" she said. "What do you feel like?"

"Not really too much right now."

"You haven't eaten since Bangkok!"

"Well, my digestive fires are not what they were in my youth."

"What's the problem?"

"I have an ulcer."

"Oh god! Is it bad?"

"It can be. I just can't eat as much as a normal person. It's not that I don't want to, I just feel full when I should feel hungry."

"Well, you should eat."

We had a couple of sandwiches and beers. When we finished we walked back up to the bungalow and sat on the chairs on the porch.

"If you could live anywhere, where would it be?" she asked, yawning and stretching her arms up over her head.

"I don't see myself ever settling into a place and putting down any proverbial roots. As long as I can remember, I wanted to ramble around with a light load and perpetual plans of moving on to the next place. The Earth is a big place, and I haven't partied with enough of its denizens yet. I want to see much more of it. And I don't see myself having a mortgage any time soon."

"How long have you been living abroad?"

"Well, I was in South Korea for two years teaching, and I've been in Southeast Asia now for...just about a year."

"Well, to be fair, after you've done it a few more years you might feel differently."

"I understand that. I mean, I don't preclude the possibility of it, I just don't see it when I look into the crystal ball of my future. And, I don't think there's some magical time when one is supposed to 'settle down' or whatever that means. I think it often means giving up your passion, your will, so you can fit into the traditional, customary role that your culture's deemed appropriate for you."

"I know what you mean. I've been traveling more or less my whole life, and I've had itchy feet for as long as I remember. But, in the past couple of years I have begun to desire a place to call home, which is kind of new for me. I want to have a wardrobe to put all my clothes in, and a garden. I've been living out of a suitcase for the better part of ten years. It's getting old. I love moving around, and everything you said about experiencing other places and cultures, but I feel like having my own home at this point. At least a base. "

I picked up a bottle of Sang Som from the restaurant and we hung out and talked through the rest of the day and into the evening, singing songs on the guitar. It was a delightful time, but before too long, I tumbled into that initially riotously fun, then slowly miasmic, dark spiral, tunneling down into the swamps of my psyche that inebriation so often compelled me to drown in.

I went to the dark place.

Of the end of the night I remember little, besides her storming off the porch several times, and cursing to myself and drinking more. I couldn't remember going to sleep.

Chapter 20

The next morning I awoke to see her looking through some papers, on her way out the door. She saw me stirring and said "I've got to go send some emails for work" and walked out. She was pissed off.

I groaned and laid there for a second while a sick feeling slowly enveloped me. I had gotten annihilated the night before. I got up and looked out at the porch and found the bottle of Sang Som. It was empty.

"Oh Jesus..."

I couldn't remember very much of the end of the night, except for making some crazy scene and going off about a bunch of dark shit.

I was terrified that she would leave. All of her stuff was still in my bag, to my relief. Maybe this was salvageable. Maybe I could handle it. I could hear her steps on the porch and she opened the door. I was sitting on the edge of the bed.

"Elena, it's like..."

"I'm not going to be stuck here in this incredible paradise with someone who has to start drinking the moment they wake up and then have a total freakout. No way."

"Elena, please. Just please don't leave, you know? Please, just sit down."

"Do you know how difficult it was last night to be here with you? Luckily I was able to keep you in the room with your crazy psycho talk. You were scary last night, Ian."

"How? I've never been violent..."

"No, you weren't violent, but you looked like Satan or something. You really did. It was in your face and in the way you were talking. You've got a seriously dark side to you man, some really dark stuff in there."

"Like what?"

"You were going on with all of this stuff about mind control and the C.I.A. and assassins and how they microchip people and send them out on missions to do all these things for all these shadowy groups that rule the world. You wouldn't stop with it, and were channeling some pretty heinous energy. I thought you were going to have a total explosion. It was scary."

"I've spent too much time staying up all night inhaling conspiracy theory websites. That stuff gets lodged and built up in there. I've thought I was going crazy myself with it before."

"It was exhausting, but what was I supposed to do? Leave you here? Then you would have gone completely off the wall. I didn't want the rest of the people enjoying this place, which I hold dear, to be inflicted upon by your drunken, raging idiocy. Its one thing to go off about something but you became downright beastly."

"Ok. Please just take it easy..."

"I mean, do what you like. But if you want to drink your way through the entire day, I'll just be on the first boat back to Koh Phangan, that's all."

I was silent.

"I mean, it's one thing to go out and get pissed, but drinking a whole bottle of rum the first night you're here is something else."

"I know. You're right."

"Well, I would love to be here with you. I would be gutted to part ways with you. But it's just not the kind of time I want to have out here."

"Ok."

"What do you mean, ok?"

"I'll take it easy, you know? I'll try it out. I've wanted to shift away from it for a long time, believe me. It's going to be a radical daily change, but I always knew it would be. I can't think of a better situation to try it out in."

"Well, I'll be here with you. This might be a good time to reappraise some things in your life. I need to do the same. We can focus on that."

I sat there for a few minutes while she had a shower.

"Are you hungry?"

"God, yes."

"Ok, let's go down and get something to eat!"

* * * * * * * * * *

We passed the afternoon like that, on the porch, passing back and forth enthusiastic and hilarious stories from our lives. I hadn't laughed like that in ages. After a while we went down to get some dinner, then went swimming.

This was all very unlike anything I had thought was possible, or available to me. I didn't think things like this actually happened. It was like that psychedelic sense that the grass is really, really green or that the floor is really, really wooden.

"Wow, look at the moon. It's so full!"

"Beautiful."

We waded into the water and clouds of florescent lights followed every movement of our legs through the water.

"Holy shit! I've never seen this before!"

"This is so gnarly..." I pushed out into the water, creating psychedelic trails behind my arms and legs under the moon's reflection.

It was the most precious, most radiantly mirthful moment of my life. It was like every difficulty, every heartache, every maddening night awake slamming my head against the wall, frustrated at all the things that made no sense to me on this planet, fell perfectly in line behind me as we pushed forth into the sacred present.

"You think they can swim up inside of us?"

"Haha, no I hope not."

"That would be trippy, to have all these little phosphorescent shrimp swimming around inside of you."

Our limbs tangled in an undulating, florescent envelope, like a force field.

"We've known each other for four days now, and I feel as if I've known you my whole life."

"I know, it's uncanny, like returning to a past life, or entering a parallel life, or stepping through a dream and it keeps going after I wake up."

I looked up at the moon again.

"I've never had any past life recollections of any kind. I've heard people talk about them a million times but I've never experienced anything I could call that. But after the first day that we were together, I felt like the only way I could make sense of how I felt around you was that I had known you before..."

"I know, Ian. When we sat down at the table together on that first night, at the lobby at the guesthouse, I felt as if you had just popped out to get something at the store or something, that you had always been there, but were just out for a minute..."

We floated and bobbed about under the moon, the shrimp sending waves of light away from our kicking legs. Untangling and swimming to the shore, I moved my legs around in the water to watch them light up one last time before we climbed back onto the sand.

Chapter 21

I woke up the next morning and laid still, my eyes resting on the trees slowly moving in the breeze outside of the window, relishing the rise and fall of her body against mine with every breath she took. She was the most beautiful woman I had ever imagined I would ever see. We held each other, basking in the vibrations. She began to wake up.

"How about I run down and get you a smoothie, and some food?"

"Oh that is sweet of you..." she yawned and stretched her delicious form. "No, I'll come down. We can go for a swim first."

"Alrighty," I said, getting out of bed and putting on my trunks.

I began doing some yogic stretches as she got up and put on her swimsuit.

"Yoga?"

"A light hatha yoga routine is necessary after waking. I am not prepared for the day without it."

"You do that every day?"

"Pretty much."

* * * * * * * * * * *

As they brought the coffee and smoothies over she mentioned that her ticket to Vietnam was for the day after tomorrow. I loathed to think that we would part, but deep down, I didn't think it was going to happen. However, I can't stand it when people try to influence my comings and goings, and I wanted her to make that decision on her own. Besides, it was quite a bit of cash.

"Well then that means we'd need to leave tomorrow, to make it on the night bus."

"I don't want to leave you..." she reached across the table to touch my hands.

"I don't want you to, either, but I want you to do what you need to for your business, and I don't want to influence what you do."

"I know..." She looked out at the sea. "Well how about we go back to Bangkok anyways, and I'll have time to think about it on the way."

"That seems sensible."

We ate and returned to the porch.

"One of the nicest things about being out here for me is that I can't check the news. I mean, its a blessing and a curse, but it's definitely new for me to take a break from it for more than a day."

"Really?"

"Yeah I'm a total info-junkie when it comes to the news. I need to know what's going on throughout the day. Its the first thing I think about when I wake up in the morning. I need to go to like ten different news websites and check everything. Many people I've known have thought it was a little over the top, even bothered by it, but I have to."

"Why is that?"

"It's like being a family member in the waiting room of a hospital, who perks up to get any news from doctors or nurses walking by. That kind of thing. There's an odd obsession I have with this planet. I need to know what is happening on it. It's beyond just a passive or academic kind of interest. I hardly ever like what I find out, but nevertheless I have to know."

"Well, this should be a nice change."

"Yeah...I don't want to 'veil my vices in virtuous words' here, but I've always thought that it had a lot to do with how much I drank."

"I think all of that has to be balanced with other, more positive information. If you're just stewing in news about wars, famines, shootings, and economic depressions, it's going to drag you down, you know?"

I sipped the mango juice and she continued.

"I think a lot of people are feeling that...what you said about it causing you to drink. I think it's a symptom of the times, I guess. And, I think we're experiencing maybe too much of the wrong kind of proximity with one another, and the planet as a whole with all of these things like smartphones and the internet that we're constantly connected to."

"Yeah...I've thought for a while, that there are positive and negative aspects to it. In a way it's like the Panopticon."

"What?"

"It's a kind of circular prison design that enables the guards to see all of the prisoners without any of them seeing the guards. But the word also implies a device which allows someone to see everything, which is a positive thing. It's like we're all in this gigantic system, and we can see everything, I guess, but it can see everything about us. So, there's good and bad aspects to it. On one hand, we can look up any information we want in the whole world, basically. I mean, if I'm struck with curiosity about Balinese marriage customs, quantum physics, crop circles, or medieval magic, I can look all that up in one second on the internet. That's incredible, truly a giant leap forward for the species. But at the same time, everything about us is tracked and monitored. So, we're at this extremely heightened state of evolution with all of this connectivity, and there are pros and cons.

"Take Facebook. In decades past, groups like the FBI had to actually go to the trouble of making a file on you, sending out agents to monitor you to find out who your friends were, your interests, clubs you belonged to, what you did with your day, where you shopped, etc. Now, we all make our own little files for them. On the other hand, Facebook is fantastic because my friends live all over the world at this point, and I get to see what they are up to."

She sat up "A weird thing also is there's those companies that have made chips to put under the skin of people or animals, that most people would never allow themselves or their kids to get, because its supposedly like the 'the mark of the beast' or whatever. But, every cell phone has a tracking device in it, and practically everyone on the Earth at this point has a cell phone, and no one seems too bothered by that."

"I know...what I see coming out of all this is a kind of spiritual vacuity. And by 'spiritual' I mean that integral sense of connectedness we all can tap into. It's ironic that we are all connected up to the gills with all these gadgets, but people seem less personally connected, like when you look at families sitting in a restaurant, and each of them has some kind of glowing, rectangular device they are completely immersed in. I fear that a kind of lower echelon connection is replacing a higher."

"Yeah...and I think that we've lost a lot of connection to the planet, to old things, to quieter things, to powerful things. To things that exist deep within us that take silence, stillness, and an inward focus in order to be more aware of. I don't think it will be that long until people as a critical mass start to feel this void in their lives, and begin to turn away from all this technology. I mean, its already happening in many places. I think we are seeing maybe two paths of evolution happening, like in one sense we are getting 'smarter' and progressing, but in another we are completely losing a kind of intelligence that keeps us living, keeps us connected to one another, and attached to the Earth as we have to be to survive."

"I agree...it'll be interesting to see where all of it goes in the next several years. As the Chinese saying goes, 'may you live in interesting times.' And these couldn't be more interesting times."

* * * * * * * * * *

I didn't want to bring it up nearly as much as I was thinking about it, but it was strange to have gone several days without any alcohol. What was most strange was that it was manageable. I didn't feel like pulling anyone's face off, and I didn't freak out. It didn't overwhelm me, it didn't turn me into a monster the way I assumed it would. It would have been extremely difficult under other circumstances, and Elena, for one reason or another, had an ability to put me at ease. She brought it up a few times, but it was easier to not talk about it. I had no idea how it would end up, or how I would feel in the coming days, but for the time being, it wasn't anything resembling the hell ride I had always figured it would be.

Sure, there were occasional cravings, but I had gotten over the initial, physical demands of withdrawal. During that time, my sweat smelled like toxic waste, and we had to change the sheets every other day because I would saturate them with foulness.

The most important difference was that I was with someone who wasn't drinking, and who didn't care to all that much. Most of my good friends had known me as the guy with the cocktail, cavalier and crazed. For years I had dealt with difficult emotions with the wishful whims of whiskey. I had never gone through the several day cycle of sweating it out of my system before. I had never drained the pool.

I had had so many fears about what I must be like as a sober person. I figured I would be disagreeable, unfunny, prickly, lobsterish. Spending those days and nights with Elena, I was able to slowly let those fears waft away from me, and it came as a mild shock to find that I still had a personality. In fact, that personality was more observant and found more hilarity in the world than it had when I was constantly staying wasted, regardless of how much laughter there had been then.

I just didn't want to be consumed by it anymore. I wanted to be concerned with other things, things that made me better, things that sated my desires and curiosities without being drowned in the rush. I didn't want to go from being obsessed with drinking as a drunk to being obsessed with drinking as a sober person. I wanted to move on from that part of my life and concern myself with other things. I wanted to be over the influence.

Regarding alcohol and addiction, Carl Jung said that they were like a lower equivalent of our desire for wholeness, for union with God. Reading that turned on a light in me, and I realized what I had been seeking in all those bottles. Rarely was it merely to escape from the vicissitudes of life, but to immerse myself more deeply into the life around me. Alcohol didn't depress my system or smother anything so much as it filled me with a great symphony, made me feel like a cathedral to house the worship of the cosmos.

Of course, it was my own aberrant way of experiencing this sense of the divine, but it damn well worked enough times to keep me coming back. Filling yourself with rum to experience a oneness with all things might sound crazy to a sober person, but it happens. There was an arousal of spiritual indwelling, of divine invocation, a chorus of the seraphim that, though it was a paltry version of naturally-occurring spiritual experiences, was surely enough of a substitute for a while. For a large part of my life, it had fueled and informed my delirious desire to experience the numinous. It was just time to move on to other methods, that was all.

But, not drinking was disorienting. Which is strange in and of itself. I mean, you'd assume that it would bring clarity and straight lines, straight thinking, predictable feelings, normalcy. But it didn't, at least not for me. In fact, it was one of the strangest headspaces I'd ever been in. It was like being high, but weirder than any high I'd experienced, because it didn't stop.

I was to the point where I drank to achieve a sense of normalcy. If I didn't have any by, say, the early afternoon, it could become awfully uncomfortable. I would have to get up and walk around, I'd get weird numbness in my limbs, shaking, very easily exasperated, that sort of thing. So, it would be very strange for me to not have it. But, I always had some around. You always figure out a way to get your fix in that state of mind, because doing normal, functional things becomes very difficult if you don't.

But you also get to have that feeling after you have been itching for it all day when you get home, clink some cubes of ice in a glass, fill it halfway up with rum, the rest with coke, and lean back against the sink and let that icy salvation soothe every capillary in your body. That's a high, big time. And, the other seven you'll have before you pass out with all the lights and your shoes on are a high as well.

I was actually, oddly, not doing too badly. I never imagined I'd go that long. And, to be fair, I don't think I ever could have without being there, in that completely unexpected situation. But, it wasn't the hysterical hell-ride that I'd anticipated. Physically, I thought that it would be much worse. I thought I might have a seizure. But, I didn't feel the anxiety scraping through my veins that I'd anticipated.

I mean, it wasn't a blast not to be drinking. It wasn't necessarily like a heavy weight coming off of my shoulders. Booze was the way I always got rid of any weight, so figuring out how to do that would be an exercise in adaptability and ingenuity. But, I thought the most rational way to look at it was as a trade-off. There were fantastic things about getting plastered every day, but there were also very damaging things as well, physically, emotionally, psychologically, socially. So, pros, and cons.

The fact that it was such a consistent part of my life, and I was so up front about it, became very much a part of my identity. And, I pulled it off, for a long time. But when you are caught in the tidal system, getting yanked back and forth, you tend to not be such a barrel of monkeys when you are sober, because you're too busy jonesing your head off to cool it and be present with yourself and others. It's impossible to find humor, jest, irony, absurdity, or anything else that's truly interesting in life when you are jonesing.

Then, when you start drinking for the day, you do find that jest, that mirth, but you know all along that you can't really get it without getting your high. And, that's not really finding the mirth. I told myself for years and years that I was finding it perfectly well in a bottle of rum, but I knew that it was ball-less. Weak. I knew that I didn't have the balls to find it sober. And, that bothered me. It bothered me and I would continue drinking to dull that realization.

I was thinking of sobriety simply as a 'good idea.' It didn't have to be an end-all be-all destination, or the ultimate answer to everything, or a new identity, or anything like that. It was simply a good idea. If I'd put any more weight on myself than that, I might crumple under it. Better to have low expectations and slowly build them up. I couldn't make any promises for the future. It seemed more judicious to just...try it out.

Either way, having gotten over the several day hump, I was pleased to see that the world hadn't ended, and there seemed to be a glimmer on the horizon that I might even...begin to like it...

* * * * * * * * * *

The next morning we pushed off in the boat right after breakfast. When we got to Haad Rin, neither of us could find the return tickets for the catamaran back to Surat Thani that we'd bought in Bangkok, so we had to buy new ones and barely made the last boat. Because of this, we were just barely able to catch the last night train back to Bangkok. They were two very close calls which came perilously, deliciously close to Elena missing her Vietnam flight.

But, we made it onto the train and found the last seat big enough for two in the whole of third class. Elena managed to get her limbs squeezed in enough to put her head on my lap, and to my amazement, went to sleep for a lot of the way. I held as still as I could, listening to music, watching the rare light fly by through the window.

When we were pulling into the station at Bangkok, she decided to just go to the airport and change the ticket so that the dates were open on it. I was elated, and all the more so that she seemed excited and relieved about it. We rode back to Koh San in a taxi, both ecstatic that we'd pried away several more days together. She put her hand in mine.

"I would have been gutted if I'd gone to Vietnam. It would have been horrible. I just feel like it would have been completely the wrong decision being there when I could have been with you."

"Same here. It would have been awful. I'm sorry you had to pay that fee, though."

"Oh that's nothing. Just a blip on the radar screen," she said, looking out the window of the cab.

"Well, how many days do we have now until you have to fly back to the UK?"

"Eight. Or nine. I think nine. I'll have to check the ticket."

"Well I don't really want to stay in Bangkok that whole time."

"No."

"Let's go somewhere."

"I was thinking on the train that if I didn't get on this flight, we could go to Pai. Have you ever been there?"

"No, but I would love to."

She turned around in the back of the taxi to face me, filled with enthusiasm that blew all of the train ride's discomfort and morning's frustrations out of the air.

"We've got to go to Pai. Besides where we just were, it's my favorite place in Thailand. It's completely different, though. It's a really artistic and gentle place, and we can do all sorts of detoxing and yoga stuff there. It's up in the mountains and there's just a very elevated feel. There's all these high energy spots around there. You can go to a million beautiful beaches out here but there's nowhere like Pai. It'll be so cool, the perfect complement to the beach, and the perfect place for us to go and get in a different headspace, a much more healthy and spiritual place."

"Let's do it."

There was a zen, Taoist energy surrounding my actions throughout this whole time. I found myself to be less acting, than acted through, without doing anything to maintain or direct my actions or those of anyone else. It was like an ingratiation, being plugged into a larger process, with full consciousness of every little thing. I was flowing in the richness of the movement of that which was happening around me, without worry, want, or will. I seemed to be in the throes of a greater will.

From the day that we met and for a considerable time following, I was thinking often of the tarot card the Chariot, and of what Aleister Crowley said about that card: "therefore is man only himself when lost to himself in the Charioting." What I was experiencing was like riding in the Chariot. All the different elements of the situation were blissfully interlocked and becoming unto themselves. In that state you do not stop and you do not go, not in any way we normally think of those things. Its just a grand flowing. I didn't have to petition, pray, or push, but to play in the sacred moment I found myself in. I didn't feel as if I had merely my own energy at my disposal, but the energy of the entire universe.

Without the crack of any whip, the horses galloped on.

We took a train up to Chiang Mai and immediately found a van going up to Pai. The ride was winding and loopy, with many cows standing in the road and the detritus of recent landslides. It was a climb in altitude and when we stopped the couple of times on the way you could tell that the air was cleaner, it was cooler, and the feeling was very different from the south. Crammed up front with the driver, we shared my ipod headphones and held hands like a couple of teenagers, excited to get up north.

Chapter 22

We arrived in the evening and went on a mission to find the place Elena had stayed the last time she'd been there. She was really pounding the pavement. I would have asked her to slow down, but I thought of all the times a woman I was walking with asked me to slow down, so I bit my tongue and was grateful. That bag was getting heavier, though. We were approaching what looked like a dead end. The road basically ended and turned into a dirt path that went up into the trees.

"Are we going to some goddamn wilderness campground, Elena?"

She laughed.

"Its up here, I'm sure."

"I didn't bring my leech socks for any ten day trek. You're gonna have to pick them out of my feet."

"No, I remember now. It's through here."

The path led through the trees and I saw some lights up ahead, opening into a small area with some motorbikes parked in front of a large, ornate wooden gate. We traipsed across some gravel and up the steps into a common area, and I could see why she was so excited to get to this guesthouse. The structure was made of mud and adobe, all with rounded edges and large old planks of wood as support. The ceiling looked like it was taken from a temple, with carvings and paintings depicting different scenes from the life of the Buddha. A woman came out from behind the counter, smiling. Elena asked if we could see a room.

"Yes, come with me, please."

We walked through a small, mazelike courtyard dense with trees and wooden statues. Each room was its own little wooden structure, and they looked like they had just been built, but with materials from hundreds of years ago, impressively preserved. Elena turned and grinned at me as the woman unlocked the door and turned on the light inside.

"Oh this is beautiful..." she said, walking slowly into the room.

It looked like a temple built for two. One of the walls was unfinished concrete that juxtaposed nicely with the other walls and floor, made of massive pieces of old wood. There were flowers and tapestries everywhere, but it had a minimal, peaceful feeling.

"Hey, check out the bathroom!"

I set the bag down and followed her in. It had an open roof, with sloping ledges of concrete covered in glass mosaics. The shower was open, and all of the finishings were modern, with stainless steel and blown glass light fixtures. There were no windows, only wooden shutters you could move to the side. It was the most impressive room I'd ever seen. Elena was in hog's heaven. I thought of the pisstank we'd stayed in the night before in Bangkok and how she hadn't said a word about how dumpy it was. I loved her so much for that, seeing how adaptable she was, yet knowing exactly what she wanted.

"How much is it?"

"How long will you stay?"

We looked at each other and shrugged our shoulders, wishing it were years.

"Probably five or six days."

"Four hundred baht."

"How about three fifty?"

The woman smiled. "Ok."

I couldn't believe it. It was roughly eleven US dollars.

"Kop kuhn ka."

"Kop khun ka." She gave us the key and shuffled out of the room, gently closing the doors.

Elena sat down on the bed and laid down, putting her arms out to me. I walked over and climbed in next to her. We laid there for a few minutes, listening to the bugs singing outside of the windows, holding one another.

"I think we're the only ones here." She whispered.

I took a deep breath. "I can't believe my life right now. I can't believe that a week and a half earlier I was in that dungeon in Korat, pacing about, with my back against the wall. I have no idea what I did right," I said, running my fingertips across the small of her back.

"I'm just glad I met you when I did." I could feel her smile against my chest.

* * * * * * * * * *

We walked back down the little trail leading to the small, two lane main road towards the center of town. The half-moon illuminated enough of the countryside to see the rice fields that lay between the hills and mountains beyond. Dozens of huts and rice barns were scattered near thin canals snaking throughout.

"What do you want to eat?"

"Anything sounds good. I think we should really eat super healthy though. I feel like just heading straight into a detox regimen."

"Oh I remember this place."

We stopped and flipped through the menu in front of a cafe with a mammoth selection of teas along the wall and a large collection of books.

"It looks uber-healthy. Perfect."

"Yeah, you think so?"

"Definitely."

We sat up in a little alcove on some cushions, surrounded all round by shelves of books, looking at the menus.

"Alright what's gonna just flush out that chemical spill musk..."

"This here's called the 'health salad.' I think that'd be a safe bet."

"Yeah...garlic, tofu, chillies, spinach, almonds...your body's going to be so relieved, Ian."

A waitress came by and Elena ordered everything.

"Hey look, there's guided meditation sessions here in the mornings, upstairs. We should go."

"Yeah, I'd like that. Although I haven't ever done that stuff in a group."

"Why?"

"Oh I don't know. People can be so pretentious about those things. I've practiced meditation and yoga on and off for years, but I don't really like doing that stuff with anyone. It feels like posing."

"Well it doesn't have to be."

"You're right. I think it's a weakness of mine, really. I mean, I think of it the way Jesus talks about prayer in the Bible, like not doing it on the street corner so everyone can see, like the hypocrites."

"That's not the same thing as going to a meditation session."

"This is true. I just never wanted to like, use that stuff as part of my identity, or to prop up my ego, you know?"

"Ok, well don't."

"I know but, so many people do."

"That shouldn't really matter."

"I guess it's just always been a way to keep blinders on, to not get distracted by other people. I mean, there are all sorts of trickeries the ego can get up to in the guise of ostensibly doing work to dissolve it. I guess I always saw the potential for that kind of trickery within myself when it came to things like yoga and meditation, which have become so commercialized and infected by superficialities. It's those kinds of things which I think turn a lot of people off to the really positive work of mind and self-examination."

"Well I understand, but I think you could get yourself pretty distracted by all that, and lose the plot yourself."

"True..."

The food arrived and we practically licked the plates it was so good. After we paid the bill and walked out into the street, the sound of a woman singing "Time After Time" came from down the road.

"Remember that? We sang that together at the beach!"

"Do you wanna go see some music?"

"Yeah! I haven't seen any live music in ages!"

"Ok there's this really cool bar that has music every night. I hope its still there."

We walked through the town and I felt like a million dollars. I should have been worried sick about my bank account and what was going to happen after she went to Hong Kong and other things like that, but they all seemed far away. I knew that feeling wouldn't last forever but I was surely enjoying it while I could. Being with Elena, just knowing that she existed, gave me comfort and peace. She wasn't worried about a thing. And neither should I have been. All that really seemed to matter was that we'd met. Everything else could get sorted out on down the line.

We approached a bar on the outskirts of town with a big sign from an old gas station. It looked rustic. There was a band playing inside, and mingling out front were longhaired Thai guys wearing denim jackets, tassled jeans, and cowboy boots.

"Oh shit...is that John Denver?"

We stepped inside the open air seating area and it was really hopping. On a stage at the back of the place was a drummer, two guitarists and a bassist playing "Take Me Home, Country Roads" while a drunk and raucous audience sang and clapped along. I immediately began belting it out, and we made our way over to a small unoccupied couch just off the side of the stage. When they finished the number I clapped louder than anyone, my enthusiasm a poignant 'thank you' to the band. They smiled and bowed, looking absolutely ripped out of their minds.

"Do you want a drink?" I shouted.

We hadn't had anything to drink since that morning at the beach, and I could tell that she wanted one, but didn't want to do anything to throw a stumbling block in my way.

"Its alright!"

"You sure?"

"Positive."

"Alright, I'll have a Chang!"

I grabbed us a couple of beers and came back to the couch. We had the best seat in the house. They began playing "Wish You Were Here."

We sat there for another hour or so and had a couple more Changs until the band took a break. We decided to head back to the room and be in the quiet together.

* * * * * * * * * * *

"I think this thing might be for good." I was shuffling around the room, looking out the open windows onto the rolling rice paddies and the smoke from the fires of palm detritus snaking up around the mountains beyond. I began to make Elena a cup of tea and myself another one. She was just waking up.

"What thing?"

"This thing. You and I. We're not just gonna be Facebook friends."

She laughed and sat up in bed.

"No."

"I think we can pull this off."

"I'm glad you think so," she said, smiling with happy morning eyes. "Where do you think you'll be?"

"I have no clue. Somewhere in Asia. I have to figure that out."

"It'd be nice to find somewhere we both want to live."

"I know..."

"I wonder when my Australian visa's gonna come through, or if it ever even will...at this point, I'd almost rather set my sights somewhere else."

I stood and looked out the window and she sat on the bed, neither of us speaking for a moment.

"It's just weird. I haven't been with anyone in so long, and...here we are. We just...need to be up front with each other. I mean, I've always felt like I was in good hands with you, but it's good to be on the same page."

"I agree."

"I'm just long over hooking up for a few weekends with someone who mildly interests me and doesn't annoy me too much just to have somebody to walk around with, where I'm unsure if I'm allowed to call or not, all of that business. I'd much rather go to sleep and wake up alone. In fact, for the past several years I've developed a pretty hardened cynicism towards the whole endeavor of finding someone I loved to be with, who really lit my fire. At the time that I met you, I was nowhere near a place where I thought I would meet someone like that. It wasn't in the cards, at least not the ones I thought I was holding."

"I was kind of in the same boat, Ian. For a long time, I hadn't felt like it was going to happen, and I was probably happier alone than being in just an emotionally dependent situation. I always wanted to find someone I could actually grow with, someone with the same morals and values, who viewed life as an opportunity to learn the *big* lessons. I want to be with someone who is passionate about what they do, and lives each day as if it's their last, and I suppose that's what I saw in you, what I liked about you when I met you. You weren't caught up in any of the normal bullshit. You had a determination, you had a mission. I mean, perhaps you were about to give up, but you still had a mission. Everyone else in the room seemed like they were just fumbling around aimlessly, but you had a drive. Even if it was misdirected. It drew me to you."

She finished her tea and I took the cup to make a new one.

"Well I think that having a partner allows us to explore ourselves in hopefully more creative ways than when we are alone. I know, perhaps now only intuitively, that there are things wrapped up within me that cannot be unfurled until I experience certain emotional states with a woman. And I think that to have a full life, a rich life, means going to those places, turning over stones and holding discarded, repressed parts of me up to the light, and putting them back together, back in the right place they need to be for me to move forward."

"Yeah."

"And, I want to be there in that way for another person. I *want* to be an agent of evolution for others, especially those that I love the most. I have desired this for as long as I remember. Of course I want to party and romp and burn the world down with infernal fun alongside a beautiful woman that I love, but at the heart of it must be this understanding, this purpose."

"I think that its a lack of that understanding, that purpose, that can drive two people apart who actually do love one another. Its just a kind of mindfulness that's necessary."

"I totally agree."

"Well I'm really glad you feel that way, Ian. I'm glad you know what you want. It's rare, and refreshing."

We sipped our tea while the Frangipani trees outside the wooden shutters ducked and swayed in the breezes of a light, mid-morning rain, my favorite time of day.

* * * * * * * * * * *

We spent six days in Pai eating greens, brown rice and tofu, going to sweat rooms, meditation sessions, cruising on motorbikes through rice paddies, examining our natal chart compatibilities, and relishing in our sparkling union. We spent every night at Buffalo Hill on that couch beside the stage.

Far from the excesses of anxiety and uncertainty that accompany meeting a new lover or partner, I felt the effluence of having found a partner with whom to ride roughshod and regaled through the exploration of life's mysteries. I was no longer riding with the ghost of remorse and apocalyptic visions of the future, but a human who made me feel like the Earth was none other than a splendid place to be.

I saw in her a life-long friend, in whom I could fearlessly confide my gem heart, my peculiarities, and all my joy and pain. Our union was a fertile plain of fun, an ambling path of self-exploration, an enflamed license to gallop on and on through the triumphs and tragedies of life.

I had always longed for a brave co-conspirator, a woman who took my preconceived ideas about life and love, shook them in her hand, and threw them across the board, giving rise to countless new vestiges from which to see the mysteries of life.

There's the idea of the alchemical marriage, which of course doesn't refer to a literal marriage of two people, but of that essentially between the masculine and feminine within each of us. Carl Jung proposed the existence of a feminine element, or aspect within men, called the anima, and a masculine within women, called the animus. Jung was very fascinated and informed by alchemy, and found an incredible amount of analogs between his unfolding understanding of the human psyche and the alchemy of mystics and visionaries from East and West. As the model of a marriage connotes, the idea is to unite these masculine and feminine elements within.

And in occultism, the universe that we conceive of is composed, basically, of dualistic energies. The Chinese provided us with the symbol and philosophy of yin-yang to express this. The masculine, in somewhat simple terms, is that which is assertive, logical, outward-facing. The feminine is receptive, emotional, inward-facing. We also find this in the symbolism of the elements. Fire is essentially masculine, where water is essentially feminine. In the universe without and within, the masculine and feminine do not correspond literally to men and women, although we are a kind of physical derivation of these energies. They are inherent in all of creation, and each of us, man, woman, or transsexual, are composed of both. The idea is to marry them, combine them, to enable a working harmony between them.

All of this filled my head while we were romping about, exploring the side roads, dirt paths, and tea houses of Pai, taking in the pristine scenery.

The precious present was our talisman of faith that in a world of seven billion people, there are those out there who complement us like a key to a lock.

The day was approaching quickly when we had to be back in Bangkok for her to get a flight to the UK for her friend's wedding. We had learned that this thing between us was something that would stick for a long time, and it was with a surprising lack of anxiety that we planned, in the last days, how we would see each other again.

"What are you going to do, Ian?"

"I have good friends in Taiwan, and I can definitely get a job there. I think that's the best option right now for me."

"That works out really well, actually. The flight from Taiwan to Hong Kong is tiny, and after I get back from the UK in a couple weeks, I'll probably be there indefinitely. I'll be able to come see you over there often."

She wrapped herself around me and buried her face in my neck.

"I want to hang out with you forever..."

"Same here, baby. We can make this work. I know we can."

"I think we can as well."

"And we have all the time in the world to figure out something more permanent. It's still early, we need to remember through this. It's best to try and be as practical about it as we possibly can."

I bought a ticket to Taipei that afternoon and we had one last evening in Pai before the next day when we'd get another night bus back to Bangkok. As Rupert had said, it was a sweet ride.

* * * * * * * * * *

At the airport in Bangkok, we waited through the precious last moments before she had to go through security.

"Meeting you has been the most wonderful thing that's ever happened to me, Elena. I've never felt this at home on the Earth, and I've never been this excited to be upright and breathing. I know we will see each other very soon, and in the meantime we'll be able to process all of this. You are the most special person in the world to me, and I can't imagine spending my days with anyone else. I felt that from the first day. Thank you for being so wonderful. I am infinitely blessed."

"I will be counting those same blessings every day...so grateful for them. We can Skype as soon as you get settled at your friend's place in Taiwan. Before we know it, we'll be back in each other's glow."

"I will always love you, Elena."

"I will always love you."

Knowing it was time for her to go through the gate, we pulled apart and I looked into her eyes again. Instead of the sadness of parting, I felt expansion, relief, joy. Having met her, I felt like I was really on the right planet, for the first time.

She walked through security and I waited until she made it through, all the way until we couldn't physically see one another.

Chapter 23

When I was going through customs in Bangkok, I was politely notified that I had overstayed my visa by a moronic seventeen days. The fee was 200 baht/day, equaling 3,400 baht, or roughly $113. Also, roughly seven more dollars than I had in my pocket. Going into gonzo survival mode, I took immediate appraisal of the contents of my bag, the only valuable item being one of those Samsung Galaxy tablets. The kindly and amused immigration officer watched my bag while I dashed back out to the ticketing area, assuming the demeanor of a circus barker. The ladies at the Thai Airways desk took sympathy with me and began barking for me.

After several frenetic moments, thinking of just how screwed I'd be if I didn't sell it, missed my flight, and was still stuck in Thailand with a higher debt, two young Thai women came forward with reluctant interest. I started at 2,000 baht but was haggled by desperation down to 1,500. I dashed back to customs with my total of 5,100 baht, gave them their 3,400, and boarded the flight.

After sinking into my seat, I counted my remaining 1,700 baht, and cursed the loss of a couple of naked pictures I'd had of Elena, that I just remembered were still on the tablet. They were priceless. The plane and the seatbelt sign were off, and despite my lowly straits I was still feeling infinitely blessed from meeting this woman.

I landed at Taipei and changed my baht for roughly $50. I was going to have to pull some Jesus-feeding-the-multitudes magic with those bills. The bus from Taipei, at the north end of the island, to Kaohsiung, at the south end of the island, was $4. An American woman on the bus let me use her Taiwanese phone and I reached my friend, who texted his address and said he and his girlfriend would be waiting up with plenty of bottles of wine. In Kaohsiung the taxi cost $2, bringing me down to $44.

When I arrived Conor lurched across the lobby, shouting "THERE he is!" We had a bro hug.

"That's the good craic."

"Mighty fine to see you, man."

"Get on upstairs! We got your room all ready."

The three of us stayed up through the night, talking about everything that had happened in the year since we'd seen each other. It was incredibly good to be with them. And I still had that blessed glow, which prohibited my lack of cash from burning a hole through my stomach lining.

The next morning, he and his lady returned and started to put breakfast together, and told me about a job interview they had just been to. It was for three open positions in Shandong Province, China, paid airfare with return, paid accommodation at a hotel, paid breakfast and dinner, plus $2,000/month. For 20 hours of teaching a week. And they needed someone pronto.

The next day we went back to the school and I was also offered the job, to which I asked "when can I go?" The woman was so delighted I thought she was going to fall out of her seat. Over the course of the next several days, the school booked my flights and the three of us sat around all day and night in their swanky apartment, catching up, laughing till we were sick in the loins.

There had to be a stop in Hong Kong in order to get the Chinese visa, but I was able to again avert disaster when the company fronted me $200 after I insinuated my penury. On our last night in Kaohsiung, we combed through the sea of food stalls at the night market and watched Conor eat bizarre and menacing creatures. My cash was now replenished to the total of roughly $220 but I knew Hong Kong would be bloody expensive just to bum about in for two days, besides the cost of the visa.

Undaunted and half crazed at this point, I got up at the crack of dawn the next morning and we said our goodbyes (they would arrive in China a few days after I did). When I got to Hong Kong I shelled out $10 for a bus ticket to the city and walked around until I found the Chinese embassy. My flight to China was in two days so I had to get next day service on the visa, which costs Americans $140. This, plus the photos I had to run out and get last minute, brought my reserves down to roughly $50, and I still had two days and nights until my flight to Jinan International Airport. I was coasting on fumes.

That day I did nothing but walk around Hong Kong, trying to take in as much as I could while I was there, getting free cups of water at Starbucks and eating from the day-old racks at bakeries. I knew that the bus back to town would cost me $10. I walked and roamed and rambled. As night descended I began to stake out a place to sleep. If only Elena had been in Hong Kong and not England for those two weeks! Heading up into the slightly less stacked-upon hills over the bar districts, I slumped past countless financiers belting back $9 Guiness pints and patting their bellies, red-faced and talking about portfolios, indexes and returns.

But, I was in love, and that love would make a softer pillow than the finest silk of any loom.

A church beneath an overpass had a spacious campus of grass and several good perches to remain unseen. I crept into a spot beside an ivy-covered storage shed and got situated. It was with a blissful gaze that I watched the stars and felt the grass underneath, falling asleep easily. The next day I stood up, saw that the coast was clear, took a piss against the shed, and walked off the grounds of the church as if I lived there.

Terrified that for some reason my visa would be rejected, destroying this golden goose egg of a plan, I waited in line at the embassy in the line you wait in to wait in another line, picked a number, my name was called, and the woman shoved my passport into my trembling hands and called the next person.

I still had another day to explore Hong Kong, an idea I wasn't riveted by. After draining the days' hours in bookstores, I decided I would just sleep at the airport. I would face less potential molestation and proselytization there, sprawled on the benches in the air conditioning, than at the church. I got the $10 bus back around midnight, claimed a nice corner, and stretched out to read my book. I had twelve hours.

It wasn't bad at all! They have benches there that are just as comfy as any hippy pad couch, and people kept a wide berth. I finished my book and loitered in the bookstores after they opened at 6am, catching up on details of salacious celebrity romances. Finally I boarded the plane and took account of my cash. $11.

I had no idea what kind of place I was headed for this three month contract. All we could gather about the hamlet of Gaoqing from the internet at Conor's place was the illustrious fact that there was a lake, populated from time to time by a swan. I looked out the window with crazed anticipation for the next chapter of this absurd adventure.

When I landed at Jinan, I was greeted by an extremely energetic Chinese man in his sixties, who would be my boss and handler for the next three months. We shuffled through the parking lot to the car through the delightfully autumnal, heavily polluted air of north western China. While we were cruising through the corn and cotton fields along the Yellow River in the fading daylight, I mentioned in a circumspect way that I was, for all intents and purposes, flat broke. He whipped around, beaming, and exclaimed "SURE! DON'T WORRY SO MUCH! RELAX AND ENJOY THE RIDE, BABY!"

Printed in Great Britain
by Amazon.co.uk, Ltd.,
Marston Gate.